"Time travel, ancient legends, and seductive romance are seamlessly interwoven into one captivating package."
–*Publishers Weekly* on *Midnight's Master*

"Dark, sexy, magical. When I want to indulge in a sizzling fantasy adventure, I read Donna Grant."
–Allison Brennan, *New York Times* bestseller

5 Stars! Top Pick! "An absolute must read! From beginning to end, it's an incredible ride."
–*Night Owl Reviews*

"It's good vs. evil Druid in the next installment of Grant's Dark Warrior series. The stakes get higher as discerning one's true loyalties become harder. Grant's compelling characters and continued presence of previous protagonists are key reasons why these books are so gripping. Another exciting and thrilling chapter!"
–*RT Book Reviews* on *Midnight's Lover*

"Donna Grant has given the paranormal genre a burst of fresh air..."
–*San Francisco Book Review*

ALSO FROM DONNA GRANT

DARK SWORD SERIES

Dangerous Highlander
Forbidden Highlander
Wicked Highlander
Untamed Highlander
Shadow Highlander
Darkest Highlander
Dark Sword Box Set

ROGUES OF SCOTLAND SERIES

The Craving
The Hunger
The Tempted
The Seduced
Rogues of Scotland Box Set

SHIELD SERIES

Dragonfyre (connected)
A Dark Guardian
A Kind of Magic
A Dark Seduction
A Forbidden Temptation
A Warrior's Heart

DRUIDS GLEN SERIES

Dragonfyre (connected)
Highland Mist
Highland Nights
Highland Dawn

Highland Fires
Highland Magic

SISTERS OF MAGIC TRILOGY
Shadow Magic
Echoes of Magic
Dangerous Magic
Sisters of Magic Box Set

ROYAL CHRONICLES NOVELLA SERIES
Dragonfyre (connected)
Prince of Desire
Prince of Seduction
Prince of Love
Prince of Passion
Royal Chronicles Box Set

MILITARY ROMANCE / ROMANTIC SUSPENSE
SONS OF TEXAS SERIES
The Hero
The Protector
The Legend (June 27, 2017)

HEART OF TEXAS SERIES
The Christmas Cowboy Hero (October 31, 2017)

STAND ALONE BOOKS
Mutual Desire
Forever Mine
Savage Moon

ANTHOLOGIES
The Pleasure of His Bed
(including *Ties That Bind*)
The Mammoth Book of Scottish Romance
(including *Forever Mine*)
**Scribbling Women and the Real-Life
Romance Heroes Who Love Them**
1001 Dark Nights: Bundle Six
(including *Dragon King*)

Moon
STRUCK

A LARUE STORY

NEW YORK TIMES BESTSELLING AUTHOR
DONNA GRANT

This is a work of fiction. All of the characters, organizations, and events portrayed in this novel are either products of the author's imagination or are used fictitiously.

MOON STRUCK
© 2017 by DL Grant, LLC
Excerpt from *Dragon Burn* copyright © 2017 by Donna Grant
Cover design © 2016 by Leah Suttle

ISBN 10: 1942017375
ISBN 13: 978-1942-17370

Available in ebook and print editions

www.DonnaGrant.com

ACKNOWLEDGEMENTS

There's no way I could do any of this without my amazing kiddos – Gillian and Connor – thanks for putting up with my hectic schedule and for knowing when it was time that I got out of the house. And special nod to the Grant pets –Sheba, Sassy, Diego, and Sisko – who love to walk on the keyboard or demand some loving regardless of what I'm doing.
Last but not least, my readers. You have my eternal gratitude for the amazing support you show me and my books. Y'all rock my world. Stay tuned at the end of this story for a sneak peek of *Dragon Burn*, Dark Kings book 11.5. Enjoy!

xoxo
Donna

Chapter 1

March
Outside of New Orleans

THERE WERE MONSTERS IN THE DARK. MINKA HAD KNOWN of them since she was old enough to understand that there really might be something beneath her bed.

Of course, growing up in New Orleans, those monsters lived beside her. That didn't make them any less scary. In fact, it made them more so. To see them interacting with others as if they were normal human beings when they were anything but...

The same could be said of the witches. Only within the last year had she come into her power, but that hadn't made life easier. In fact, it had made it worse.

Minka had been lied to by her coven and then given to the most heinous monster of them all: Delphine. The Voodoo priestess was on a quest to gain as much power as she could, in whatever way possible.

It was only by the skills of the LaRues that Minka was alive. The werewolf pack policed New Orleans, keeping the supernatural world in balance.

After her escape from Delphine's clutches, Minka had taken refuge and found solace at her great-aunt's home in the bayou. It had been willed to her after her aunt died, and Minka had never thought to actually use it.

Had her aunt foreseen such events? Had she known it would be the only place for Minka?

She stood in the open doorway and looked out over the bayou. The moon was hidden by clouds, giving the land an ominous feel.

A soft splash to her left alerted her to an alligator. And in the distance was the soft howl of a wolf. The Moonstone pack had returned to the area, and their numbers were growing steadily.

The darkness was where evil liked to hide. It was why most people feared it. It was partly because they couldn't see, but there was another part that knew there were unspeakable horrors awaiting them in the shadows.

Whether that was from their ancestors' fears or encounters, she didn't know. It wasn't a learned trait. Instead, it was something people were born with.

One prime example was Delphine. On the streets of New Orleans, everyone shied away from the Voodoo priestess—locals and tourists alike. It was as if everyone could sense the malevolence within her.

Minka took a deep breath, enjoying the quiet of the evening. She wasn't sure how much more she'd get before Delphine came for her. But unlike the other monsters, Delphine wouldn't wait for the night to strike.

Once before, the priestess had attempted to kill Minka in an effort to take Minka's power. There had been a short period after her escape when no one but the LaRues knew where Minka was hiding out. All that had changed when she helped Court LaRue and Skye Parrish fight against the djinn and vampires.

Minka had shown herself to her enemies, but there hadn't been any other choice. Her friends would have died without her, and she couldn't allow that.

That had been six months ago. Every day that passed without Delphine coming for her only made Minka more nervous. Some might take that to mean Delphine wasn't interested.

But Minka had looked into the priestess's eyes. She knew that Delphine had marked her. That kind of stain didn't ever go away. Delphine could come for her in the next ten minutes, ten months, or ten years—but she *would* come.

Movement out of the corner of her eye drew Minka's attention. She walked to the screen covering the porch and looked down from the stilted height of the house to see an animal moving among the bushes.

She caught a glimpse of white fur, her heart kicking up a

notch as she wondered if it was Solomon. Then the werewolf moved into the clearing, and she saw that it wasn't solid, silvery white as Solomon was. She waved when the werewolf looked up at her. The Moonstone pack had been good about watching over her, and they'd become her friends.

Minka didn't want to think about her disappointment at the wolf not being Solomon. It wasn't as if he checked in on her at all. As the eldest LaRue, his domain was New Orleans. He didn't have the time to think about her—nor would he. He didn't like her.

Which both rankled and hurt her because she liked him. A lot. She didn't want to. In fact, she'd tried to hate him, but that hadn't turned out well. All it had done was make her crave him more.

It was awful to be attracted to someone who couldn't stand your very presence. She didn't know why Solomon detested her, and it didn't matter.

So what if she'd warned Myles of his death.

So what if her magic had removed the silver from Myles's system and saved his life.

So what if her home had been used in the vampire/djinn war.

So what if in an effort to save the LaRues, their women, and the Moonstone pack, she had shown herself.

The LaRues had rescued her from Delphine's clutches.

In her book, she'd never be able to repay them for that. And she didn't worry about the fact that they'd probably done it because Delphine had Addison, as well, and since Myles had fallen in love with Addison...nothing would come between a wolf and his mate.

It didn't matter why Minka had been saved, only that she had. She had come into her magic then, and she was a force to be reckoned with. Every day she pushed herself to her limits to train because every little bit would help when Delphine came for her.

Minka rubbed her tired eyes. She was only dozing a few minutes every hour. The last thing she wanted was to be caught sleeping when the priestess arrived.

The sound of her cell phone vibrating on the table had Minka turning and entering the house. She picked up the phone to see it was a text from Addison asking if she was all right.

Addison and Skye sent her texts daily to check in on her. Minka had made them promise to stay away until Delphine was taken care of.

Minka sent a quick response and replaced the phone on the table before crawling into bed. There were wards up all around the house. They wouldn't stop Delphine, but they would slow her. And that could be the difference between life and death.

She shut her eyes for a moment, intending only to rest. Almost instantly, she was drifting in that space between sleep and wakefulness.

Suddenly, her mind screamed for her to wake, alerted that

someone was in the room with her. Her eyes snapped open as she jerked upright to see a figure standing in the wide doorway leading out to the porch.

"Easy," said a male as he lifted his hands.

Minka blinked, recognizing the voice. She relaxed as Griffin, leader of the Moonstone pack, lowered his arms to his sides. "What are you doing here?"

"I've been knocking at your back door for ten minutes."

She glanced at the clock to see that she'd been asleep for two hours. "Is something wrong?" she asked as she rose from the bed.

"Not at all. I thought you might like some company."

It was then that she realized he was naked. Thank God the lights were out. Or perhaps, she should wish they were on to get a better look at his fine body.

Minka knew Griffin was interested in her. If only she returned his feelings. It would be so much easier than this thing she had with Solomon. Truthfully, it wasn't a thing. It was nothing.

"You've not left this house in six months," Griffin said.

She shoved back her wealth of curls from her face. "Not true. I walk along the bayou sometimes."

"You know what I mean."

"I do. I also know there are five witch covens out there, some of which helped my coven turn me over to Delphine. I've no desire to fight those witches when I need to save myself for Delphine."

"Who says you'll have to fight the covens?"

She shot him a look. "Seriously? Do you know anything about witches?"

"Very little, actually."

"Well, let me fill you in. They all hate me. That's insanely idiotic since they're the ones who turned on me, but they'll be gunning for me because Delphine has told them I have more power than they do."

He crossed his arms over his chest as he leaned a shoulder against the doorway. "Then why haven't they come for you?"

"Because they fear Delphine. They know she's marked me, so until I beat her, they'll keep their distance."

"Do you think you can best Delphine?"

She looked at Griffin's face, hidden by the shadows of the room and shrugged. "I'm certainly going to try."

"What a woman you are."

As compliments went, that was a nice one. "Thanks."

"Come walk with me."

"You're naked."

A laugh rumbled from his chest. "I didn't take you for a prude."

"Oh, I'm not."

"You just don't want to see me naked."

"I didn't say that."

"You pretty much did."

She threw up her hands in defeat. "It's just...weird."

There was a beat of silence. Then Griffin said, "That's the

first time I've ever had a woman say my nudity was weird. Most throw themselves at me."

"I'm not most women."

"And that's why I want you."

He'd let his interest show many times, but he'd never come out and been so blatant about it. And she was very flattered. There was something sexy about a man who wasn't afraid to go after what he wanted.

Griffin dropped his arms to his sides. "Say something."

"What does one say after something like that?"

"Anything."

She walked to stand beside him at the double doorway as she looked outside. "You say you want me, but I have to wonder how smart that is."

His head turned to her. "Why?"

"Delphine has your sister. She'll use Elin to get to me through you." Minka didn't add that she might already be doing exactly that. She wanted to think of Griffin as her friend, an ally—not an enemy.

He pushed away from the door and faced her. "My feelings have nothing to do with my sister or Delphine."

"It wouldn't be wise to test things. You're gathering your wolves again. The Moonstone pack was once one of the greatest in the area. Your wolves will expect you to find someone within your pack, not a witch."

"I don't give a shit what they want."

She smiled at the Alpha coming out in him. "You're my

friend, Griffin. One of the few I can count on. You and your pack have kept an eye on me, and for that, I'll be eternally grateful. And yes, I'll walk with you."

"But you won't be mine."

"I'm thinking of you with my decision. Your pack might accept me as your casual lover, but never more than that. And you know I'm right about Delphine. She'll find out. She always does. You returned to New Orleans for your sister. You'll do anything for her."

"Minka—"

"We never know what we'll do for family, and we both know what Delphine is capable of," she said over him.

He blew out a breath as he looked at the sky and the hidden moon. "That bitch needs to die."

"I agree."

His head swiveled back to her. He gently tugged on a curl and released it, watching it spring back into place. "I'm going to come for you every night for a walk. And every night, I'm going to ask you to be mine. I care about you, Minka. I have feelings for you."

She took his hand in hers and smiled. She didn't need the light to know that his green eyes were alight with determination. It was in his words, his touch.

"Let's walk," she said.

It would distract her from her worries for a little while. And perhaps that's exactly what her mind needed.

Chapter 2

Gator Bait Bar
New Orleans

"Someone has to check on Minka."

Solomon was inspecting the food and handing it to the waitresses to serve while Addison and Skye were behind him, nagging. And they were fucking good at it.

"I don't have time for this now," he told them. "Come back after the lunch crowd."

Skye stepped in front of him, her dark eyes holding his. "We've been trying to talk to you about this."

Solomon looked around for his brothers to help, but the three of them were out in the bar, tending to customers.

He turned to grab the next plate to inspect, only to find Addison in his way. She had her arms crossed and a blonde brow raised as she glared at him.

"It's been six months," she said.

Had it really been that long? The peace that had come after the battle with the vampires and djinn had been blissful. Everyone knew it wouldn't last, but Solomon loathed doing anything that would see it come to an end even quicker.

But he had to get to work.

"Fine," he relented. "I'll check on her."

With a smile, the girls sauntered off.

It wasn't until the lunch rush was over and Solomon walked into the front to see Addison, Myles, Skye, and Court sitting together waiting for him that it struck him—he'd been set up by the girls.

"So, they finally cornered you," Kane said as he came to stand beside him.

Solomon swung his gaze to his younger brother. "Shit."

Kane's lips twisted as he shrugged. His blue eyes—the same eyes all four of the LaRues had—pinned him. "I expected you to hold out longer."

"They were damn smart to come at me during the lunch hour when I was too busy to deal with things." Solomon ran a hand down his face, furious with himself for not seeing the girls' ploy.

"Is it really so bad?"

He frowned at Kane. "Is what so bad?"

"Going to see Minka? She's very pretty, and a powerful ally."

"Then why don't you go to her?"

"Who says I haven't?"

That set Solomon aback. "When did you go?"

"She risked her life for Skye. Not to mention Riley."

No sooner had Kane said her name than their cousin walked into the bar. She waved to the others and came to stand beside him and Kane.

"So," she said looking between them. "You're talking about me, huh?"

Solomon shook his head. "How could you possibly know that?"

"It's the looks on your faces," Riley stated. Then her gaze slid to Kane. "Have I told you how much I hate the DMV? I'd have renewed my driver's license online, but noooooo. I had to update my stupid picture. As if anyone ever takes a good picture there. They set you up to fail. With glee in their eyes, I tell you," she said and walked around them to the back.

Solomon watched as she sauntered away, still grumbling, and walked through the doorway into the kitchen. He hadn't exactly been thrilled when Riley had shown up. Partly because she'd run from her brothers and didn't bother to tell them she was in New Orleans.

Now that the Chiassons knew, things hadn't gotten easier. Mostly because they were so intent on hunting the paranormal in Lyon's Point that they'd forgotten their baby sister was a grown woman who could make her own decisions.

That's what she was doing now. Making her own decisions. And it was killing the Chiasson boys.

Solomon had never been so glad he didn't have a sister as

he was at that moment. Riley was a true blessing, but he'd be a wreck if she were his sibling.

Yet, she'd done wonders for Kane. Solomon glanced at his brother. The messy, always late Kane was now quiet, withdrawn, ten minutes early for everything, and never had a hair out of place.

That's what happened when you pissed off a Voodoo priestess who then cursed you to hunt down someone. With their cousins' help, Solomon had prevented Kane from killing while in wolf form. Had Kane killed anyone, he would've remained a werewolf, never able to shift back into a human.

And he'd have gone mad.

Delphine's little experiment had changed Kane in ways none of them understood. Solomon saw the visible signs, but there were ones deep within Kane that he kept from everyone. Except for Riley. If he shared anything, it would be with her.

The two of them had gravitated to each other. She healed him, while allowing him to play protector. Their bond of friendship was strong.

Blood tied their two families together, but it was the interaction that allowed such bonds to develop and strengthen the ties.

Friends and allies were the same. Addison and Skye were right. Someone should go see Minka. He briefly thought of sending Kane, but he'd told the girls he would go. So he would.

And the sooner he got out there, the quicker he could get

back to the bar.

"I'm glad to see you've given in to the inevitable," Kane said.

"Yeah. I'm heading out there now. I'll be back in a couple of hours."

"Take your time," Kane said as he walked behind the bar and began to clean up.

Solomon nodded to Myles and Court before walking into the kitchen and then out the back door. He locked the wooden gate behind him and got into his truck.

On the drive through New Orleans, he looked for any signs of Delphine or her followers. They were easy to spot since they were usually in all white. There were times he saw them watching the bar.

It wouldn't surprise him to find one of them now. The fact that he saw nothing made him uneasy.

Six months. Six idyllic, heavenly months where the supernatural had been reminded of the strength of the LaRues—and obeyed the rules.

It wasn't easy policing the streets of New Orleans with all the different supernatural beings that called the city home. But it was what his family had done for generations. And they were damn good at it.

Solomon wasn't sure who had it the worst. Was it he and his brothers monitoring and patrolling the city? Or was it his cousins who hunted and killed the supernatural that were drawn to Lyon's Point?

Once out of the city, Solomon turned up his music and tried to relax. But the closer he got to Minka's, the tighter his muscles became.

By the time he pulled up to the house, he was contemplating turning around. Before he could change his mind, he threw the truck into park and turned off the engine.

In his mind, he was running through hundreds of reasons anyone other than he should be there. Yet he found himself out of the truck, and his feet kept taking him toward the stairs regardless. When he reached the steps, he planted one foot on the bottom rung and hesitated.

Some might think the bayou was quiet compared to the city, but it was anything but. There was a cornucopia of animals who called the swamps home, and their sounds filled the air like a mystical symphony only those who appreciated it could hear.

It was a place that suited Minka. She was the embodiment of stillness, of calmness in the loud, frenzied city. Not that he would ever tell her such a thing.

He felt eyes on him and looked around until he spotted the werewolves in the bushes. Somehow, he wasn't surprised that the Moonstones were still watching over Minka.

His gaze jerked to the house. Would he be interrupting her and Griffin? The thought brought a smile to his face as he headed up the stairs to the front door. Though he didn't allow himself to think about *why* intruding on the two of them made him happy.

But as he raised his hand to knock, the door swung open. Minka stood there in jeans and a cream sweater that accentuated her mocha skin, the evidence of her Romanian Gypsy heritage.

For a long minute, they stared at each other.

Her long, curly, dark brown hair hung loosely about her shoulders. Eyes pale brown and ringed with black watched him without guile from beneath insanely long lashes. Her lips were wide, the bottom slightly fuller than the top.

She was a natural beauty with skin that was as smooth as silk. His gaze traveled down her slim neck to find a collarbone bared from her wide-necked sweater that hung seductively and alluringly off one shoulder. Faded, ripped jeans clung to her legs, but it was her bare feet with their dark pink-painted toenails that he found intriguing.

Then she stepped back and motioned for him to enter, which jerked him out of his thoughts.

He looked around the house, noting that she hadn't changed much since the last time he was there. "How've you been?"

"I'm alive. I think that says it all," she replied.

"Yeah." He cleared his throat, not sure what else to say.

She closed the door and stood there, examining him. "I talk to Addison and Skye every day through text. You didn't have to come, especially since you obviously don't want to be here."

"I never said that."

She snorted loudly. "I hate to be the one to break this to you, but everything you feel or think is shown through your eyes. I don't know who made you come—"

"No one," he interjected.

"But you did. You came, you saw, and we spoke. Now you can leave with a clear conscience."

He pointed at her. "This. This right here is why I didn't want to come. You twist everything."

"Really? So you came on your own? No one told you to?"

Solomon opened his mouth, then shut it.

"That's what I thought," Minka said with a smug expression. "I'm not angry, if that's what you think. You did this for your family."

"And for you."

The words were out of his mouth before he had time to think about them.

Her brows rose, surprise in her eyes. "I admit, I'm surprised you'd say such a thing. I know how you detest me."

"I don't hate you."

She gave him a wry look. "Your actions and words say otherwise."

"I have a lot on my plate." It was a poor excuse, but it was the only one he had.

It wasn't as if he could tell her that she made him uncomfortable—and all too aware that it had been years since he'd tasted a woman's kiss or held a female in his arms.

"Are you really all right?" he asked.

Her gaze lowered to the ground, and he saw something flash in her eyes before she hid it. "Yes. Griffin and his pack get me whatever I might need."

"But?" Solomon pressed.

She took a deep breath and then slowly released it as she met his gaze. "It's the waiting that's killing me. I don't know why Delphine hasn't come for me."

"Don't think that way. Take this time she's given you."

"My power has grown," Minka said. "But I could train and practice for ten years and still not be ready. She's more powerful than I am."

Solomon took a step toward her. "Don't think like that either. You must stay positive. Believe you can win."

A smile turned up her lips. "You're right. I should, and I will."

Silence once more descended upon them. Solomon was trying to think of something else to say when the sound of footsteps coming up the stairs had Minka looking out the window.

There was a smile on her face when she opened the door to allow Griffin inside. He held several bags of groceries in his hands and he came to a halt when he spotted Solomon.

"I didn't know you were stopping by," Griffin said.

Solomon shrugged, glimpsing the flowers half-hidden in one of the bags. He was sure Minka hadn't asked for those. "Just wanted to check on things."

"It's only taken you six months."

Griffin's dig riled Solomon. Then again, two Alphas visiting the same woman had that effect. Solomon's suspicions were confirmed. Minka and Griffin were together.

Why then did he feel the need to fight Griffin?

Solomon ignored him and looked at Minka. "Let us know if you need anything."

He shouldered past Griffin only to have Minka put her hand on his arm. Solomon turned back to her.

"Thank you," she said softly.

He gave a nod, and then her hand was gone.

And damn if he didn't miss her touch.

Chapter 3

Solomon had barely reached the bottom of the steps before he heard Griffin shout Minka's name. Without a second's hesitation, Solomon turned and took the stairs three at a time.

When he reached the top, he found Minka's eyes had gone milky. "No!" he shouted when Griffin made to touch her. "She's having a vision."

"What do we do?" Griffin asked worriedly.

"Nothing."

Griffin ran a hand down his face. "I've never seen this."

Neither had Solomon, but Myles had explained what happened when Minka had had such a vision with him. Solomon couldn't look away from her eyes.

No longer could he see the pale brown irises. She made no sound or movement as the vision held her in its grip. He stayed near her in case she collapsed, yet all the while, he wondered what it was she saw.

Suddenly, her chest expanded as she dragged in a ragged breath. Her lids closed on a blink. As he watched, the milky color vanished as if it had never been.

Her eyes fastened on him a second before her knees buckled. Solomon grabbed her the same time Griffin did, and together, they walked her to the couch where they sat her.

Solomon reached for the glass of iced tea on the side table and handed it to her. She drank it down as if she hadn't tasted anything in weeks. He squatted beside the sofa, and when she finished, he took the empty glass to set it aside.

"What did you see?" Griffin asked.

Solomon shook his head at the werewolf. Now was not the time to ask such a question. Minka would tell them in her own time—if she told them at all.

She put her hand to her forehead and closed her eyes while laying her head back on the cushion. Solomon had never realized that having a vision took so much out of her. Then again, he'd never witnessed it before.

"Rest," he told her as he straightened and made for the door.

Solomon grabbed Griffin's arm as he passed, dragging him with him. Once outside, Solomon shut the door behind him and motioned with his chin for Griffin to head down off the porch. When he hesitated, Solomon raised a brow. Finally, Griffin relented and started down the stairs.

Solomon's thoughts were on Minka while he followed a

few steps behind Griffin. It was because of that, that he didn't see Griffin's intention as he pivoted and slammed his hands into Solomon's chest.

Solomon stumbled back a few steps before a wooden pillar holding up the house stopped him. He glared at Griffin. "What the fuck is your problem?"

"You've got some nerve coming here."

Solomon smiled coldly and then pushed away from the stilt. "Worried I might be encroaching on your woman?"

"Leave."

"No."

Griffin's eyes flashed yellow, a sign that he was fighting to remain in human form. "She doesn't need you."

"That's not for you to decide."

"It's not yours either."

Solomon shrugged and circled him. "If you were secure with Minka, you wouldn't be worried about my arrival. Which means, the two of you aren't a couple."

"Yet."

"Be that as it may, you don't get to tell me to stay away. Minka is our friend. We watch over our friends."

Griffin's lips curled into a sneer. "Tell me, Solomon, why then did it take any of you six months to visit? Where have you been all these weeks as she remained hidden behind the walls of her home?"

"Keeping New Orleans in order. Or did you forget my family has an obligation? Just as yours did."

"You son of a bitch!" Griffin yelled as fury contorted his face. "You just had to bring that up."

They were circling each other now, each looking for a weakness to exploit.

Solomon shrugged. "I'm sorry if you don't like being reminded of the cowards your parents were. Perhaps if they'd done their job, a duty that had been bestowed upon your pack for generations, then my parents might still be alive."

"You don't know that."

"Permission for your return to this area has been granted by me. Remember that."

Griffin bared his teeth. "And remember, we can leave at any time."

"You're good at that, so it doesn't surprise me that you'd throw something like that in my face. You returned to New Orleans to take your rightful place, and you were doing a good job."

"You don't like being questioned," Griffin said with a taciturn smile.

Solomon saw members of the Moonstone pack watching them, but he didn't give a shit. "Your fur's all ruffled because I came to see Minka. If you want to make this about something else, I'll happily indulge you."

"You've still not answered why you're just now showing up."

He'd had enough. Solomon closed the distance between them until they were nose-to-nose. "Because Minka asked to be alone. She wanted the time to herself, and we gave that to her. In case you didn't know, we spoke with her every damn day. And I know Kane has been here."

Griffin's hands were fisted at his sides. "Kane runs with us, yes."

"Anything else you want to accuse me of?" Solomon demanded.

"A call or text isn't the same as visiting. We've watched over her, brought her what she needed, and offered her company. Whatever obligation you believed you had is long gone. Leave."

There was only one person who could tell him to go. Minka. Solomon made as if he were turning away, but instead, delivered a solid punch to Griffin's jaw.

The next instant, they were locked together, each trying to get an advantage over the other. Solomon blocked punches while connecting more hits. A blow to his mouth split his lip, blood filling his mouth.

He ignored it and elbowed Griffin in the nose. The sound of cartilage breaking filled the air. Solomon then found himself on his back after having his legs swiped from beneath him. He raised his arms in an X to block a downward kick to his face. Grabbing Griffin's foot, Solomon shoved him away, twisting the other man's leg so Griffin spun in the air.

Solomon kicked up to his feet and tried to ram his knee into Griffin's face, but Griffin blocked him. Instead, Solomon slammed his fist down between Griffin's shoulder blades.

Griffin bellowed in pain. His head jerked to Solomon, and without any warning, he shifted. Solomon stared at him, even as Griffin snapped his jaws toward him.

"You're a were by birth," Solomon said. "Your ancestors chose this life and passed the gene down to you. If you can't handle a situation in your true form without shifting, then you're not the werewolf Kane told me you were."

Griffin growled, his lips peeled back to reveal his large teeth. He crouched low, his muscles tense and ready to pounce.

But Solomon didn't move.

He wasn't afraid of Griffin. Not now. Not ever. New Orleans was his and his brothers' to protect by birth and by right—and that included any allies and friends.

"You want to sever the tenuous pact we have," Solomon said. "Then attack."

Griffin suddenly took a step back. Solomon turned his head and found Minka walking toward them.

She stopped between them, looking at each of them a long moment. "Enough of this."

"The sooner we get this done, the better," Solomon said.

A dark brow rose as her head turned to him. "Not here. I need to think about my vision, and I can't do that with the two of you making all this racket. I need you to leave." Then she looked at Griffin. "Both of you."

Without another sound, Griffin loped away.

Solomon watched him, knowing that they would clash

again. It was the way with two alpha males. It was one of the reasons Griffin's parents had failed Solomon's, because the elder LaRue hadn't addressed a similar issue.

Solomon wouldn't make the same mistake. Though once a great man, his father had grown lax at the end, believing the reputation of the LaRues would keep them safe. When Delphine had come for them, the Moonstone pack abandoned them.

Solomon didn't just have his three brothers and his cousin Riley to look out for anymore. He also had Addison and Skye. Six people were under his care, and that meant he couldn't fail.

Not as he'd done with Misty.

He swallowed. The thought of his dead fiancée always hit him hard. It didn't matter how many years passed, he would always carry the weight of her death with him.

Solomon wiped the blood away from his mouth and glanced at Minka. "I apologize."

"It's what two Alphas do, right?" she said with a small smile.

He nodded and turned his head to spit out blood. "You know we stayed away because you asked us to."

"I do."

"We shouldn't have."

She wrapped her arms about her middle. "It was my request, and you honored it."

"Promise you'll call one of us if you need something."

"I won't," she said with a shake of her head.

"Minka..." he began.

She took a step back, her gaze halting him. "Don't. You know why you can't be here. Delphine has already damaged Kane with her curse."

"That we got her to reverse."

"You're not a fool. You know as well as I do that she's not finished with your family. Especially Riley."

He didn't need to be reminded of the Voodoo bitch's attention to his cousin. Delphine had already tried to harm the Chiassons before, but no one knew why she was so focused on Riley now.

"The more distance you put between yourself and me, the better," Minka said.

"United we stand. Divided we fall."

She gave him a sad smile. "Then what I just witnessed with you and Griffin says it all, doesn't it?"

"I won't fail in this. I can't," he told her.

"Some things are out of our control."

He nodded slowly in agreement. "You're our friend. Not only did you save Myles, but you also helped us in the last battle. The LaRues don't forget things like that. I don't care who or what is coming for you, Minka Verdin. We look out for our friends."

"United, huh?"

"United."

She blew out a breath. "I'll contact you once I've pieced

together what the vision has shown me."

"Come with me to the city." He wasn't sure why he offered, only that he wanted her with him.

"I can't."

"You can. When was the last time you had a meal you didn't cook? Or got any sleep. I didn't want to mention the dark circles under your eyes, but I will if it means you'll come with me and get a good meal and some sleep surrounded by those who can protect you."

She glanced at the ground. "I am protected."

Griffin. Right. How could he forget that? "I can't change your mind?"

"Not this time."

Even he had to admit defeat. This time. But he'd be back with reinforcements to help make a case for her to return with them, if just for a night.

"Be safe, then."

Minka flashed him a smile. "You, as well, Solomon."

He held her gaze for a long while before he turned on his heel and walked to his truck.

Chapter 4

WAS IT WORSE TO WANT SOMEONE YOU COULDN'T HAVE? Or to never know that kind of longing?

Minka wasn't sure which was more awful. She knew that no matter how much she hungered for Solomon's touch or craved his attention, that she would never be his. That kind of knowledge did strange things to a person.

Her heart had jumped in her throat to find him there. It had felt like forever since she'd seen his face and those brilliant blue eyes. All the LaRues and Chiassons had them, but Solomon's were brighter than the others'.

And his hair. The dark blond strands were laced with pale brown that made her want to sink her hands into the locks.

His face was all hard angles and ruggedness that she longed to touch and kiss. The shadow of dark whiskers on his jaw made her stomach flutter and her skin prickle with awareness.

Then there was that body of his. Could anyone wear

jeans like Solomon? The denim clung to his trim waist and hips, curving over his fine ass before encasing his long legs. Though it was his ability to wear a plain white shirt over the impeccably hard sinew of his chest and wide shoulders that could make her heart miss a beat.

He was simply mouth-watering. The complete package... and utterly out of reach.

But there were other things she needed to put her mind to. Like deciphering exactly what she'd seen in her vision—and figuring out just what it meant for everyone.

She couldn't do that with Solomon there because every time she looked at him, she saw an image of Delphine standing among dozens of dead weres as she laughed.

Without looking in the direction Griffin had walked off to, Minka turned and made her way up the stairs and into her house. She shut the doors and walked to the middle of the living room.

She sat in the center of the oval, braided rug in shades of cream, brown, and orange, and with her legs crossed and her eyes closed, she concentrated on her breathing.

With each inhale and exhale, her body relaxed, and her mind calmed. Only then did she call up the images of the vision. The first was of Griffin in wolf form. Solomon was next, the platinum fur of his beast unmistakable.

Next came more werewolves. There were so many images, flashing rapidly for what felt like years. So many that she couldn't distinguish one from the other. But the howls, yelps, and growls all pointed to one thing: fighting.

What she couldn't determine was who the werewolves were battling. Or even where.

That was important information. Without it, it was almost pointless for her to tell anyone what she'd seen in the vision. Because those snippets could mean absolutely anything. It could happen tomorrow or a year from now.

Minka took a deep breath and slowly released it as she came to the next images. Just thinking of Delphine caused her to tense, so seeing her in the vision sent Minka's heart rate skyward.

It took every ounce of her meditation skills to keep herself calm. Only with a tranquil heart and quiet mind would she be able to accurately determine what the images in the vision meant.

Once she was ready, she let the first imagine of Delphine fill her mind. The Voodoo priestess was in all white as usual, her long, black hair in dozens of tiny braids falling to her hips. She was standing tall, her gaze straight ahead—almost as if she were looking right at Minka.

Delphine's lips were moving, but Minka couldn't make out the words. The next scenes were of the streets of New Orleans, littered with dead werewolves. Everywhere Minka turned, there was one carcass after another.

Then she saw him. Solomon.

His silvery white fur covered in blood drew her. She studied the image closely, noting that he lay dead outside of

Gator Bait with his three brothers around him.

If only that were the extent of the killings. She saw Skye lying within feet of Court. Here and there were humans who had gotten in the way during the battle.

But nowhere were there witches, djinn, or vampires.

Delphine entered the vision again, her laughter loud and boisterous as she walked among the dead werewolves, her white clothes splattered with blood. Her arms and face were coated with it, as if she'd smeared it over herself.

When Minka thought she'd looked at that image long enough, she moved on to the last one. The cemetery. She knew the place all too well since it was where Delphine had tried to kill her and Addison to enhance the priestess's power.

And in the vision, Delphine managed to do just that with Addison. There was a burned body next to Addison, and Minka could only guess that it was her. But it was difficult to say without seeing anything to identify the body by.

One thing was for certain—everyone she knew and cared about was dead by Delphine's hand.

All Minka wanted to do was put the vision out of her mind and forget it, but her gifts had given her a glimpse into the future for a reason. Whether she liked it or not, she had to glean every last drop of information from it.

She went through each scene thrice more, filing away small things she hadn't noticed before. Only then did she finally stop at the image where Delphine was moving her lips.

Minka replayed that scene over and over, deciphering first

one word, then two, and so on until she finally figured out what the priestess said. Minka's eyes flew open, a chill racing down her spine.

They were words she would never forget.

Look hard, Minka. This is all because of you. You're responsible for the slaughter of the weres. You're the one who got your friends killed. This is just a taste of what I have planned.

Minka put her hands behind her neck and leaned her head back, stretching the muscles. She was chilled to the bone by those words. There was no escaping them, however.

She got to her feet and looked outside to see that it was dark. A quick glance at the clock showed she'd been meditating for seven hours.

For months, she'd hidden away in the bayou, hoping that Delphine might forget her and move on. Minka had foolishly thought if she kept the LaRues away, that they might not suffer backlash from Delphine.

All of it had been for naught.

Minka couldn't keep what she knew to herself. Everyone needed to know so they could prepare. She picked up her cell phone and sent a text to the LaRue brothers, Addison, Skye, Riley, and Griffin, telling them to get to her house immediately.

Then she walked out onto the porch and gazed out over the bayou. The tranquility she'd sought—and found—there was gone. Perhaps it had all been in her mind anyway. She knew how far Delphine would go to get what she wanted.

"Minka."

She looked down to see Griffin staring up at her. She gave him a nod, and he hurried up the steps.

"What is it?" he asked.

She remained looking out over the water. "I only want to say it once. Let's wait until the others get here."

"It's nighttime. It's Gator Bait's busy time. It'll be hours before any of them are here," he said.

An owl hooted nearby while the frogs croaked loudly. She looked to find the bird of prey and spotted him as he flew from a tree, swooping down to catch his dinner.

"I don't care how long it takes the others to get here," she said. "We wait."

"Walk with me," he urged.

She glanced down at the hand he held out beside her. Her gaze lifted to his face as she forced a small smile. "Perhaps later."

Griffin let his hand drop to his side. He then walked away without another word.

She knew she'd hurt him. It wasn't her intention, but she didn't want to be with him. She wanted...it didn't matter what she wanted. She wouldn't be on this earth long enough to do anything about it anyway.

To her surprise, she heard the sound of a vehicle approaching. It wasn't long before the engine cut out and the vehicle door opened and closed. Then a second car could be heard.

Though Minka wanted to rush to the front of the house to see who had come, she remained where she was. The first ones to come into view were Riley, Skye, and Addison.

Her friends ran up the steps and threw their arms around her, all talking at once. There hadn't been another time when she'd felt so loved. She drank in the feel and sounds of her friends. It wasn't until they were there that she realized just how much she'd missed them. Talking on the phone or via text just wasn't the same.

She stepped back, her gaze drifting downward to land upon Solomon. Their eyes met, but Court soon took Solomon's attention.

"What happened earlier?" Addison asked in a whisper.

Minka frowned as she looked at her. "What do you mean?"

"When Solomon came," Skye said.

Minka shrugged. "Nothing much."

Riley flattened her lips and snorted. "Then where did he get the busted lip and bruised jaw?"

"He and Griffin...had words," Minka finally admitted.

All three looked at her with knowing grins on their faces. She couldn't help but smile in return. They wanted her with Solomon, but she'd made sure they didn't know how much she would like that, as well.

She didn't like people interfering in her love life, and besides, if Solomon were interested, he'd have done something about it. The fact that he hadn't pretty much said it all in her mind.

Her small living room was soon filled with four men and three women besides her. She moved to the kitchen to get glasses for drinks. It wasn't until she turned to start handing them out that she found Griffin in the doorway, staring at her.

"We're all here," Myles said as he took his glass of sweet tea.

Minka wiped her hands on her jeans and stood, facing them. "Right. You are. I didn't expect you to get here so quickly."

"You said immediately," Kane replied from his position by the door with Griffin.

"Yes, but I know y'all have the bar to run."

Addison swallowed her sip of tea after sinking onto the sofa. "Solomon told us you had a vision. We've been waiting to hear from you."

"Gator Bait is tended to," Court said. He motioned for Skye to sit between Addison and Riley while he took the chair, and Solomon remained standing off to the side.

Now that everyone was there, Minka didn't want to tell them anything. They were a family, a cohesive unit that loved deeply. Their smiles would be gone by the time she finished.

Riley lowered her drink to her leg. "I see you looking at us with an anxious expression. Whatever you have to say can't be worse than what we've already been through."

"That's true enough," Skye said.

They made it sound as if they were prepared for what she'd

seen, when she knew they weren't. No one could be.

"It can if it's about Delphine," Griffin said.

Every head swung to him.

Minka shot him a frown. "How do you know that?"

"It's obvious," he said with a shrug.

A look around the room confirmed his statement. Minka licked her lips. "Fine. It is about Delphine."

"Go on," Addison urged.

Minka tried, but every time she looked at Addison, she saw her lying dead, her throat slit.

"Holding it in won't make it any better," Kane stated.

Minka closed her eyes and nodded. Then she took a deep breath. "My vision was about Delphine, but it was also about all of us. And every werewolf in the area."

You could've heard a pin drop it was so quiet after her statement. Minka opened her eyes, her gaze snagged by Solomon's. His intense blue eyes seemed to see right through her.

She wanted to shove aside the strand of dark blond hair that had fallen onto his forehead. Wanted to stand next to him and feel his arms around her while he held her close. She hadn't experienced that kind of comfort in a very long time, and she ached for it.

Minka mentally shook herself. She had to continue talking. Yet the words were hard to get past her lips. "I saw the streets lined with dead werewolves. The LaRues were killed outside the bar along with Skye and Riley. Addison, she took you to the cemetery where she...finished what she began with us."

"And me?" Griffin asked.

Minka lowered her eyes to the floor. "I saw so many wolves...I can't say for sure."

"And you?" Solomon asked.

She blew out a breath and lifted her head. "I assume the burned body I saw beside Addison is me. As horrific as all of that is, it's the words Delphine delivered that are the worst."

"Words?" Court asked.

"In one of the images, I saw her lips moving. I figured out what she was saying."

Riley scooted to the edge of the cushion. "And that was?"

"*Look hard, Minka. This is all because of you. You're responsible for the slaughter of the weres. You're the one who got your friends killed. This is just a taste of what I have planned.*"

Chapter 5

THE BLOWS JUST KEPT COMING.

A bad feeling had plagued Solomon ever since leaving Minka's earlier. Now he knew he should've stayed in the area. Not that he could've helped her. Most likely she wouldn't want him anywhere near.

"Well," Kane said. "At least we know what's coming."

Minka's eyes bugged out. "That's all you have to say? I saw your deaths."

"You saw mine before, too," Myles added.

Solomon had to admit, Myles had a point. Perhaps there was a way out of this, just as Minka had been able to draw the silver out of his brother to save his life.

"How many of the weres?" Court asked.

She shrugged. "Too many to count. They were everywhere. I've never seen so many."

Solomon looked to Griffin. "How many have joined your pack lately?"

"Fifty," he replied after a long hesitation.

Kane snorted loudly. "More like a hundred."

There was an advantage to Kane running with the Moonstones. Kane had insight none of the rest of them had. The fact that Griffin lied was something else Solomon would have to handle. The sooner, the better.

"Why would you lie?" Skye asked Griffin. "We have to work together."

"United," Solomon said and looked to Minka.

Her lips softened into a smile. Then in the next heartbeat, it was gone. "Unity is important here," Minka said.

"Is it?" Griffin crossed his arms over his chest. "From what I'm hearing, anyone associated with the LaRues will get killed. My charge is to protect my clan."

Kane faced the Alpha. "Your *charge* is the LaRues. Didn't you swear to uphold the traditions set by our families before your parents allowed ours to die?"

Solomon felt Minka's gaze on him, but he didn't look at her. His attention was on Griffin. *Sooner* had become *right now*. "I told you earlier that if you couldn't uphold your responsibility, I'd revoke my forgiveness of your pack."

"We're over two hundred strong now," Griffin stated in a terse voice. "I don't think we need you."

Court and Myles slowly rose to their feet.

It was Court who said, "Don't be an idiot. The wolves have joined you because Solomon granted your return. If he revokes that—if we all revoke it—the wolves will leave."

"Maybe," Griffin said.

Kane shoved him so that Griffin slammed back against the wall, rattling pictures. "What the fuck is your problem? I vouched for you to my family. I gave you access to return to your home and have your pack be the power it used to be."

Griffin held Kane's gaze for a long time before he shoved him away and walked out the door.

"Let him go," Solomon told Kane when he went to follow.

Myles's gaze slid to Solomon. "Are you insane? We need the weres."

"And we'll have them. I'll talk to Griffin later." Solomon glanced at Minka. "We'll stand united."

Riley crossed one leg over the other. "Well, this should be fun."

"What do we do now, then?" Skye asked.

Solomon said to Minka, "I really think you should come with us now. United, remember?"

"When was the last time you slept?" Addison asked her.

Skye nodded her dark head. "Yes. Come with us."

"It looks like I don't have a choice," Minka said.

Solomon knew her halfhearted attempt at refusing was for herself. She was a strong woman who felt she had to do everything on her own. He would show her she didn't have to.

He moved toward his brothers as the girls went to help Minka gather some clothes. While he stood with his siblings, his thoughts kept turning to Griffin and how to resolve their issue without them killing each other.

Court ran a hand through his butterscotch blond hair. "I don't know whether to be pissed at Griffin or scared shitless at Minka's vision."

"A little of both," Kane said.

Myles grunted. "Yeah. Both. I understand what you're saying, Solomon, but if we stand any chance against Delphine, we need the Moonstone pack now."

"What about the other factions?" Court asked.

Solomon rubbed his jaw. "Minka didn't mention them, and she would have if she'd seen them. That could mean they didn't take sides."

"Or they did," Myles added.

Kane looked into the bedroom and lowered his voice to say, "I think maybe we need to call in our cousins."

"I've already thought about that," Solomon admitted. "The problem is that if we bring them here, we'll be delivering them right into Delphine's hands."

"True," Court said. "But they have a witch. Davena was strong enough to stand against Delphine. She, along with Minka, might do the trick."

Solomon liked the idea, but he kept coming back to the vision. "Minka didn't see the Chiassons."

The discussion stopped when the four girls returned. After Minka had turned off all the lights and locked up the house, they walked together to the trucks.

Solomon climbed into the driver's seat of his crew cab as

Kane took the passenger's seat. A moment later, Minka and Riley climbed into the back seat. He looked in the rearview mirror and found his gaze clashing with Minka's.

"Ready?" he asked her.

She nodded as she fastened her seatbelt. "Ready."

The drive back into the city was done in silence, each of them lost in their own thoughts. There would be more discussion, but Solomon wanted it to wait until everyone had had a chance to think things through. And he wanted Minka to get some rest.

He pulled up alongside the curb of the bar and shut off the engine. They climbed out and made their way behind the bar to enter at the back.

Right before he entered the building, he glanced up at the second floor. He used the studio as a place to sleep when he didn't want to drive out to the family house. In fact, in the last six months, he'd only spent two nights each month out there. It just made more sense to remain in the city.

His gaze lowered to Minka, who was having a hard time keeping her eyes open. It was lucky for her that he had a bed close where she could crash.

Solomon entered the kitchen and walked to the front to grab a glass behind the bar, filling it with bourbon. He returned to the back and found the others in the office. Minka kept blinking to keep her eyes open, but he knew she wouldn't give in to sleep easily.

He moved behind the desk and opened the bottom drawer

where he got a pinch of the herbs his parents had used to make Court sleep when he was a toddler. Solomon had never gotten rid of them, and he was glad of that now.

After sprinkling them in the liquor and waiting for them to dissolve, he handed the glass to Minka.

She accepted it with a smile. Her exhaustion and all the conversation kept her occupied, so she didn't realize how quickly she drank it all. Solomon watched her closely. As soon as she began to sway, he took the glass from her.

She looked at it and then him with unfocused eyes. "What did you do?"

"Made sure you would rest."

"You...drugged me?" she asked in reproach, her words slurring.

He didn't get a chance to answer as she went limp against him. Solomon lifted her into his arms and looked down at her. Now that he was holding her, he wasn't so sure about putting her in his bed.

Mostly because the thought made his blood burn with hunger.

"Which of you is going to take her home?" he asked his brothers.

Myles shook his head. "I've got Addison, Court has Skye, and Riley is staying with Kane. Looks like you're the one with the room."

"You do have two places," Court added.

Damn. Solomon should've seen that one coming. He

didn't try to argue with his brothers, mostly because, by the looks of everyone in the office, they wanted him to take the witch.

Kane walked ahead of him and opened the back door. As Solomon passed, Kane said, "If it's too much, I have room for her."

His words stopped Solomon in his tracks. Too much? No woman had been inside his home since his fiancée.

"Solomon?"

He turned his eyes to Kane and shook his head. "It's fine."

"Are you sure?"

"Yeah. I renovated the upstairs a few months before Misty was killed."

Kane's gaze held his before had gave a nod. "We'll take turns watching over Minka while she sleeps."

"All right."

Solomon turned to the right to a set of metal stairs leading up to the loft. When he and his brothers had bought the building, they'd intended to use the upstairs as storage. Yet the more Solomon had thought about it, the more he liked the idea of living there.

So with some work—and soundproof floors—he'd made it his. Being in the heart of the city they protected made things easier. It was why his brothers had also each chosen a place within New Orleans.

But he couldn't give up the family house.

Solomon reached his door and adjusted Minka so he

could key in his entry. The door unlatched and swung open. He kicked it shut behind him where it automatically locked once more.

He walked to his leather couch and paused beside it, but he didn't set Minka down. Instead, he turned on his heel and made his way to the bed.

She didn't stir when he laid her down or when he removed her shoes. He then covered her and straightened. If he expected to feel something about another woman in his bed, he was wrong. There was only a twinge of pain at the thought of Misty's untimely death.

But it had been nearly seven years since that terrible night. A lot had changed since then—him most of all.

He smoothed a curl from Minka's face before he turned and walk to the kitchen area. Idleness wasn't something he enjoyed, but that left him little to do while he watched over Minka. So, he cleaned the kitchen from the mess he'd made at breakfast.

After that, he put in a load of laundry. Anything to keep from staring at Minka sleeping in his bed and imagining her naked...and tangled in the sheets.

"I suppose you've heard."

Delphine watched a passing riverboat from the dock. She didn't look toward Tora. She was devoted to her followers, but Delphine knew better than to trust anyone. "You mean that Minka is in the city? Of course."

"Why don't we attack?" Tora asked.

"It isn't time."

"We've waited six months already."

Delphine turned to the younger woman and put her hand on her light-skinned cheek. With Creole heritage, Tora was a true believer in Voodoo. She was young and pretty, if a little headstrong.

"There is a reason for everything I do. Don't question me again."

Tora's dark eyes flashed with annoyance. "I know how much you need the witch to grow your power. She was alone and weak. Now she's with the LaRues."

"Do you fear the werewolves?"

"No."

Delphine smiled as she lowered her hand to her side. "Good. They are dirt beneath our shoes. They believe they control this city, and I've allowed them that fantasy. Just as I showed their parents who was really in charge, I will do the same to them."

"Why didn't you take over when you killed the parents?"

Delphine swept her arm wide to encompass the entire city. "Everyone fears me. They know me and what I'm capable of. I've allowed the weres to handle the little squabbles while I concentrated on the bigger picture."

Tora lifted her chin and smiled. "You're a force to be

reckoned with. I can't wait until I stand beside you and show the werewolves and the rest of the factions what's in store. You will be their queen."

"Yes. And in so doing, I'll get my revenge on the Chiassons, as well. But we wait. For now."

"Not too much longer, please."

Delphine turned back to the river. "I won't mess this up, but don't worry. You won't have to wait too long."

"Do you still want us to keep watch over the LaRues?"

"I want to know everywhere they go, as well as everyone they speak to. They're not stupid animals. They'll be preparing."

Tora laughed. "It doesn't matter what they do. They'll never be prepared for what you'll bring them."

Delphine smiled. "No. They won't."

Chapter 6

Minka came awake slowly, her body relaxed and her mind calm. She stretched, yawning as she arched her back with her arms over her head. She opened her eyes and looked at the high ceiling.

That wasn't her ceiling.

She turned her head and saw a brick wall with a large picture of New Orleans at night.

That wasn't her picture or her wall.

She sat up and looked around in confusion. The loft was large with the windows letting in tons of light. A soft rain battered the glass before rivulets of water ran down to collect at the base of the window.

It took her a moment to hear the shower over the rain. She threw off the covers and noted that she was still in the clothes she'd worn when she came to New Orleans—with Solomon.

That's when it all came back to her. He'd drugged her.

Anger coiled within her like a snake ready to strike. Minka

rose and strode to the sliding barn door to the bathroom that wasn't shut all the way. She pushed it open and continued into the room where she saw the white marble counter and white-and-gray-basketweave tile upon the floor.

She ignored it as she made her way to the glass shower where Solomon had his back to her as he washed. Despite her anger, she couldn't help but notice his impeccable body through the steam and water.

Wide shoulders tapered to a narrow waist and hips. His ass was...sublime. The fact that she noticed it only pissed her off more. And yet, she let her eyes travel lower to his long, muscular legs.

It was his hands running through his hair that jerked her gaze upward to watch the way the sinew in his back, shoulders, and arms moved sensuously. Damn him for being so gorgeous.

Minka threw open the glass door. "You've got some damn nerve."

Solomon whirled around, and for a moment, she forgot to breathe. If he'd been gorgeous from the back, from the front, he was magnificent. She fisted her hands by her sides to keep from reaching out and running her fingers along his thick chest and washboard stomach.

"Minka," he murmured, a small frown forming.

She kept her gaze upward, refusing to look down and see his cock. "You drugged me."

"You needed the rest."

He stood beneath the spray, seemingly unperturbed that he was naked and she was staring. Which only angered her even more. "You had no right."

"You'd have done the same thing had I looked the way you did. You were practically falling over you were so exhausted."

She crossed her arms over her chest. Her gaze lowered for just a moment to see his flaccid rod hanging between his legs. The length was impressive, and she was disappointed that he wasn't hard.

Then she was furious with herself for looking when she'd decided not to.

"You overstepped," she stated and pivoted.

She didn't get even one step away before a large hand wrapped around her arm, immediately soaking her shirt. The next heartbeat, she was yanked beneath the spray to stand in front of him.

"What the hell is wrong with you?" she cried.

Solomon loomed over her, his blue eyes flashing dangerously. "I was saving your damned life."

"I didn't ask that of you!"

"No, because you wouldn't stoop so low as to ask *me* for anything."

"What the hell does that mean?" she demanded.

His lip curled as he snorted. "As if you don't know."

"Oh, please," she said with a roll of her eyes. "I'm surprised you put me in your bed when I know you'd rather have dumped me in an alley somewhere."

"You don't know what the hell you're talking about."

Her eyes widened. "Oh! The gall! You know exactly what I'm referring to. All those condescending remarks, the not-so-subtle way you let it be known that you don't want me around. You hate that a witch is helping, don't you?"

"It has nothing to do with you being a witch," he stated coolly.

She shoved her wet hair out of her face and blinked through the water splashing on her cheek. "So you admit you have an issue with me."

A muscle ticked in his jaw. "I didn't say that."

"You didn't have to. It's in the way you talk to me."

"You don't know what you're saying."

She'd had enough. Not to mention, she was now completely soaked. "Admit you hate me."

"I don't hate you!"

"Right," she said with a laugh. "Everybody sees it."

His eyes narrowed as he leaned closer. "You're wrong. They're wrong."

"Whatever."

"I try to do something nice for you, and you've got to throw it in my face."

She gawked at him before issuing a loud laugh. "Nice? You fucking *drugged* me!"

"For your own damn good, as I've said! Someone had to take care of you since you wouldn't do it yourself."

Her mouth fell open as his words registered. She was so

shocked that her mind went blank for a second before a dozen replies filled her. She took a breath to give him a piece of her mind when she heard someone clear his or her throat.

Minka and Solomon turned their heads at the same time to find Myles standing in the bathroom. His blond brows were raised as he glared at both of them.

"Are you two finished? Because I've been standing here for some time trying to get your attention," Myles said.

Minka looked down at herself to see her clothes clinging to her. She'd been so furious, she hadn't even realized she was still standing in the shower, completely clothed.

When she looked back at Solomon, his gaze was on her. No longer did those blue eyes of his pin her with arrogance and anger. Instead, there was remorse.

Myles pulled a towel from a hook and held it out to her. "Your bag is on the bed."

She moved to the entrance of the shower and took the towel. Then she waited until Myles had turned on his heel and left before she stepped on the rug.

Behind her, the shower cut off. She wiped her face and tried not to think about Solomon—naked—behind her.

"Stay," he said.

She stilled, unsure of what he meant.

He slid past her then. Her gaze dropped down to see his fine ass right before he wrapped a towel around his waist. Only then did he turn to face her.

"There's still plenty of hot water left," he said. "Take your time."

She watched him walk out of the room and slide the door closed behind him. For a long minute, she simply stood there. Then she dropped the towel and pulled the wet clothes from her body before tossing them into the sink to wring out later.

Solomon stood with his back against the bathroom door until he heard the water turn back on. Only then did he make his way to the armoire.

"That was some fight."

He paused in reaching for a pair of jeans at the sound of Myles's voice. "I thought you'd left."

"You should've looked around. You'd have seen I was sitting on a barstool."

Solomon blew out a breath and tossed the jeans and a black tee onto the bed. He dried off before getting dressed and facing his brother. "What do you want?"

"Oh, I don't know," Myles said with a shrug. "Perhaps to talk about that fight I witnessed where you were standing naked in the shower, and Minka was with you. Fully dressed."

"Things got out of hand."

"Well, that's one way of putting it." Myles leaned an arm on the island in the middle of the studio. "We all knew she'd be pissed when she woke."

Solomon shrugged and walked to the coffee pot where he

poured himself a large mug. "Yep."

"What now?"

"I think she'd be more comfortable staying with Riley and Kane."

Myles's lips curved into a smile. "That's what you think?"

"Yeah."

"You can be so stupid sometimes."

Solomon sipped his coffee, eyeing his brother. "Just sometimes?"

"Sometimes, you're actually smart, but this isn't one of those times."

"Gee. Thanks for the confidence."

Myles jerked his chin toward the bathroom. "You're a prime idiot when it comes to her."

"I have an idea. Why don't you tell me what you really think," he said as he set down his mug on the island and faced his brother.

"Fine. I will. You want Minka."

Solomon shook his head. "No. Yo—"

"You want her," Myles stated over him. "You try to treat her like shit in the hopes that no one—especially Minka—will realize it."

"Is that right?" It was the only response Solomon could come up with.

Myles nodded. "You know it is. You don't need to explain why, brother. I know the reason. You forget I was with you that night."

That night. No other words were needed to speak of Misty's brutal murder.

"Minka is different," Myles said. "She's strong and courageous. Not to mention, she's a witch."

Solomon ran a hand down his face. "And none of that removes the fact that Delphine is after her."

"Delphine wants us, as well."

Solomon splayed his hands on the granite of the island. "That's right. Delphine will come for us. I need to be focused on that."

"You can have some happiness," Myles said, a frown puckering his brow.

"I tried that. It didn't work out."

"You tried it with someone who didn't know who—and what—you were. Misty was a sweet soul, but she was weak, Solomon. She was delicate, vulnerable, and utterly defenseless."

Solomon knew Myles was only stating the truth. At one time, those words would've sent him into a rage. The fact that they didn't now was what angered him. "*I* was her defense."

"You didn't fail her." Myles rose to his feet and shot him a sad smile. "I know you think you did, but you didn't. It was a tragedy, plain and simple."

Solomon didn't bother to reply as Myles let himself out. For long minutes, he remained at the island, staring down at the mug of coffee.

No matter what anyone said, Solomon knew he was the

cause of Misty's death. He hadn't been there when she needed him. Of everyone, he'd known how fragile she was. It was because of that that he should've been with her at all times to prevent such an outcome.

The thing was, he knew it was a blessing that Misty was no longer alive. She'd never have accepted his world. How many times had she laughed off the stories of vampires and other supernatural creatures? It was why he hadn't told her that he was a werewolf.

He hadn't shared the truth of himself with her because he'd feared she wouldn't be strong enough to deal with his paranormal world of danger and death.

The sad part was, it was because of him that she'd been singled out—and killed. Hiding the truth hadn't helped Misty. It had only made things worse.

The shower turned off, pulling his attention back to Minka. She was the exact opposite of Misty in every way. Dark, strong, powerful, and a force to be reckoned with.

It was what had drawn him to her from the very beginning.

It was also why he couldn't allow himself to give in to the need pounding through him.

Chapter 7

Rest did wonders to reset the brain. Minka might not have wanted to admit how tired she was to Solomon, but it was obvious she'd needed the sleep.

Her stomach rumbled loudly. With the shower behind her, she wanted clothes and food. She walked out of the bathroom with the towel wrapped around her and found her bag on the bed. A quick search produced the clothes she was looking for.

Just before she released the towel, her head swung to the side at the smell of food. She spotted Solomon in the kitchen, cooking.

She ducked back into the bathroom and hurriedly changed. Then she hung up her towel and wrung out her wet clothes to dry before she made her way to him.

He glanced up at her when she climbed onto one of the stools. "That shower is amazing."

"That it is," he replied without looking at her.

She licked her lips as she eyed the stack of pancakes. "Can I help with anything?"

Turning, he set down a bottle of syrup and the flapjacks. "The plates are in the cabinet."

She slid off the stool and grabbed two plates as well as forks before returning to the island. Solomon had already placed three pancakes on her plate by the time she sat down again.

Minka was too hungry to wait. She doused the pancakes with syrup and began eating. It wasn't until she'd polished off those and reached for more that she realized Solomon was watching her as he slowly ate.

"What?" she asked around a mouthful of food.

He shook his head, swallowing his food. "I'm impressed with your appetite."

"It feels like I've not eaten in weeks." When he didn't reply, she reached for the syrup and asked, "How long did I sleep?"

"Three days."

She couldn't believe she'd slept that long. Then again, she'd gone nearly six months without a solid night of sleep. She set aside the syrup. "Well, that explains why I'm so hungry."

"I shouldn't have drugged you."

She cut into her pancake and threw him a smile. "The herbs didn't keep me asleep. My body did. While I'm loath to admit it, things are clearer now that I've rested."

"That's good to hear."

"What happened while I slept?"

"Nothing."

She finished her bite. "Nothing? That's odd, isn't it?"

"It's been like that for a while now." Solomon set down his fork and pushed away his cleaned plate. "There will be days where there's no activity."

Minka finished off her last two pancakes. She then tucked her hair behind her ear and swiveled the stool so that she faced him. His blond hair was still damp on the ends, making her want to reach up and touch it. "Do you think it's Delphine?"

"Everything is about Delphine."

"So what do we do?"

He tapped his index finger on the black granite counter. "We need to take her out."

"Can we? Everyone believes she's too powerful. Me included."

"And that power is continuing to grow. How much longer before she comes for you and Addison again?"

That thought was enough to make Minka's stomach clutch painfully. "I'm not strong enough to take her."

"Maybe not on your own."

"No." She shook her head and got to her feet, pacing away from him. "You and your brothers have done enough. And I'm pretty sure the Chiassons would rather you not involve Riley in anything."

Solomon followed her toward the sofas. "Riley is a grown woman, who will do whatever she wants. Much like you. I don't want to involve her, or my cousins. But the simple truth is that none of us can take on Delphine alone. We're stronger as a group."

"Delphine already wants each of us for some slight or another. Now you want to become a beacon for her to shine her attention on?"

He moved past her to the windows and looked down over New Orleans. "You're right. Delphine does want each of us. We can wait around and let her pick us off one by one, or we can band together." Solomon turned and faced her. "I fought against her when she cursed Kane. And I'll do it again."

"Why didn't you kill her when you had the chance?"

His gaze dropped to the floor. "I went after Kane in Lyon's Point to stop him from hurting Ava. Court and Myles were the ones who trapped Delphine here in New Orleans. It was Court who had his teeth around her throat until she released Kane from his curse—at least the changes she made to his curse. Court could've killed the priestess, but had he, the hex would've returned to Kane, and then would have come to each of us."

Minka slowly sank onto the sofa. "You didn't trap her. She allowed you to take her."

"Yes," he replied and looked at her. "We've kept that bit a secret. I was hoping I'd eventually work out the reason for Delphine's actions."

"She wanted something from you and your brothers, and since she released the curse from Kane, I'm betting she found it."

Solomon nodded. "She didn't ask a single question of my

brothers while they held her."

"Where did they keep her?"

"A warehouse."

Minka picked at a chipped thumbnail. "It wasn't LaRue property?"

"No."

"Then what could she have wanted?"

He shrugged. "I've gone over everything Myles and Court told me about that night, and I can't figure out what it is Delphine wanted or got from my brothers."

"We may never know."

"That's not an option. She killed my parents. She terrorizes those in the factions as well as humans. It's time she was shut down."

Minka said, "I'm all for that. We're going to have to be careful."

"Does that mean you'll join us?"

As if she had a choice. It was suicide to face Delphine on her own, and Solomon knew that. "I will, but I'd like to point out that anyone who Delphine hasn't already marked shouldn't be involved."

"I say we allow anyone who wants a piece of that Voodoo bitch to join in. We're going to need the help."

"And if we fail? Delphine will go after everyone who helped us."

Solomon lifted his shoulders in a shrug. "She'll go after them anyway."

"That's a lot of pressure we're putting on ourselves."

"I don't see any other choice."

She pushed herself to her feet. "You're right. We don't have one because she's backed all of us into a corner. I don't like being trapped."

"Neither does she."

"I'd like to be the one who corners her, so she has no escape."

One side of his lips lifted in a smile. "I'm sure that could be arranged."

Minka returned his smile, her gaze dropping to his mouth. It felt weird to not be bickering with him. Not that she was going to say anything to change it. But after so long of him constantly raising her hackles, she was seeing a different side of Solomon.

"What?" he asked with a slight frown.

She gave a shake of her head. "I don't think we've ever had a civil conversation before yesterday. Or rather when you came to the bayou."

"No, I don't suppose we have."

She didn't know what else to say. She glanced out the windows as the rain continued to beat upon the glass. "Thank you for breakfast and for letting me take over your bed these past few days."

"You say that as if you're leaving."

Her gaze shot to him. "I'm not leaving the city, if that's what you're worried about."

"I'd feel better if you stayed."

Her heart thudded in her chest. "Here?"

Alone, with him? Just the two of them? She wasn't certain that was a good idea. All she had to do was think of him naked in the shower to realize that.

"Here," he replied with a nod. "I'm usually always at the bar anyway, and the couch is comfortable when I do need to sleep."

Well. That's what she got for thinking—even for a split second—that he wanted her there because he liked her. It was just convenient.

"Um...all right," she relented.

"I won't bother you."

She forced a smile. "I should be the one saying that. This is your home."

"For now, it's yours, as well."

"Thank you."

He waved away her words. "You can remain up here, but you're welcome in the bar anytime. I'm sure the girls will want to chat with you."

"Let me help out somehow. I can stay in the back, but I've been idle for so long that I want something to do."

Rubbing a hand over his chin, Solomon eyed her. "How do you feel about filing?"

"It's busy work. Just what I'm looking for."

"Then come on. You're about to make Myles's day."

Minka followed Solomon to the door, a thread of eagerness

running through her. "He doesn't like filing, huh?"

"It piles up until one of us finally has enough and does it for him," Solomon explained as they walked through the door.

She heard it lock behind her as they walked down the stairs to the bar below. As soon as they entered the back door into the kitchen, the vibe of the place filled her. Music could be heard coming from the front, while the cooks were shouting orders and replies to each other.

Unable to help herself, she watched them for a moment, mesmerized by how they moved like a well-oiled machine. Each had their own station and duties, but it was the way they relied on each other that kept things moving at a steady pace.

"Still hungry?" Solomon asked from behind her.

She glanced at him as she shook her head. "I find this fascinating."

"Don't let Marcus hear you say that. He'll have you in the kitchen with an apron on before you can blink."

Minka didn't think that would be such a bad thing. Reluctantly, she turned and followed Solomon inside the office. She spotted the two tall stacks of files and documents atop the cabinets.

"I did warn you," Solomon said.

Before she could reply, Myles walked in. "What's going on?"

"I wanted something to do. So, I'll be filing," she replied.

His face lit up. "I'd kiss you right now, but I'm already taken. Perhaps Solomon could do it for me."

Minka chuckled, all too aware that Solomon was glaring at his brother. "Where do I start?"

She listened as both Solomon and Myles explained their filing system. It was simple enough, and she immediately grabbed a handful of papers and opened a drawer.

She could feel Solomon's gaze on her as he and Myles spoke about a liquor order that was due in that afternoon. Their talk soon turned to teasing as they talked about a daily pool tournament and bets on if Solomon could beat Court again.

For just a moment, Minka was able to forget that she'd been in hiding, waiting for a psychotic Voodoo priestess to come for her. That small window of time gave Minka the normalcy she'd been missing since she left the Quarter after her coven betrayed her.

The LaRues were giving her an anchor she hadn't realized she missed—or needed. How could she ever repay them?

But the answer was clear as day. Delphine. Once that crazy bitch was gone, the city could return to normal. And the LaRues wouldn't be looking over their shoulders anymore.

Chapter 8

Solomon couldn't remember a day crawling by as slowly before. And he knew the reason. Minka.

When she'd offered to help out at the bar, he'd jumped at the chance to have her in sight of his brothers. Instead, Solomon sought her out with his eyes and ears any chance he got.

"Should I ask where your head's at? Because it surely isn't here."

He looked up at Marcus, the head cook, who was also aware of what the LaRues really where thanks to Solomon saving him from a vampire years ago. "I'm fine."

"You usually lie better." Marcus handed him a basketful of fries, along with a crawfish po'boy. "Your mind is somewhere besides on the food. And I've an idea just where it's at."

Marcus glanced into the office where Minka was still filing. Solomon didn't bother to reply. Marcus wasn't just a good employee, he was also a friend. It was because of that friendship that Solomon kept his mouth shut instead of telling Marcus to mind his own business.

"She's staying with you, right?" Marcus asked.

Solomon nodded as he pulled a ticket from the line and checked each of the plates before calling for a server to deliver the food. Only then did he look at Marcus. "You can stop whatever thoughts you might be having. There's nothing going on between Minka and me."

"Perhaps there should be," Marcus said with raised brows. He nodded toward the office and winked.

Everyone wanted him to find a woman—preferably Minka. It wasn't that Solomon was against the idea.... That wasn't exactly true. He was violently opposed to the thought.

He'd already lost one woman he loved. He wasn't sure he could ever put himself in that position again. The loss has been devastating, crushing. He'd picked himself back up because he had no choice with his brothers counting on him, but he wasn't sure he could do it a second time.

And it was inevitable. All he had to do was look at his parents and his ancestors. The LaRues lived passionately, fought brutally, and died viciously.

He was prepared to do the same, but what he couldn't do—what he *wouldn't* do—was allow another woman into his heart only to have her ripped out of his grasp and killed. Even someone like Minka.

In some ways, it would be worse with her. She knew the secrets of the city because she was part of it. That meant she would be in the line of fire every time. It was simply a matter of the odds turning against her one time.

And with Delphine hot on Minka's trail, it was only a matter of time.

Though that could be said for any of them.

Solomon put Minka out of his mind and concentrated on his job. He refused to glance toward the office. And that's how he got through the next several hours.

It wasn't until mid-afternoon when things slowed that he was able to take a break. He had the night off, but now that Minka was in his place, he thought it might be better if he remained.

"I've got this," Court said as he walked up. "Your shift is over."

Solomon thought about arguing. Most likely, his brothers would think his staying was a ploy to keep away from Minka. And they'd be right. It was an argument he really didn't want to have. Ever.

With a nod, Solomon walked out the back. He stared at the stairs for a long time, trying to decide if he wanted to go up or not. Everyone thought he didn't want to be around the witch. That wasn't his problem at all. It was because he *did* want to be with her that made him hesitate.

Movement out of the corner of his eye had Solomon jerking around to find Kane pushing away from the corner of the fenced area.

"I didn't know you were there," Solomon said.

Kane raised a blond brow. "That much is obvious. Did you not tell her the code to get in so she'd have to find you?"

Shit. Had he? Was that the reason he hadn't thought about giving her the code to get into the loft? Solomon wasn't sure. "I forgot."

"I let her in a few hours ago. I like Minka."

"Everyone does."

Kane's blue eyes held his. "Including you?"

"She's a friend, so, yes."

"That's not what I meant."

"I know." And Solomon wasn't going to say more.

Kane's gaze lifted to the door at the top of the stairs. "Be kind to her."

"I am."

"You haven't always been." Kane's look was dark when he returned his gaze to Solomon. "There were times you went out of your way to hurt her. But I know the real reason."

Solomon hoped that by not responding, Kane would drop it. He should've known better.

"You treat her with such disdain because you do like her," Kane continued. "In fact, it goes beyond like and straight to attraction."

"Leave it."

"Did you leave me to deal with Delphine's curse on my own? No. You risked your life to stop me. To save me. Well, brother, I'm going to be here pushing you to the very thing you're afraid of."

Solomon blew out a breath. "Why? What does it matter what I do or don't do with Minka?"

"Because you're a good man who had tragedy strike, and that shouldn't ruin the rest of your life."

He didn't know what to say to Kane. In fact, all Solomon could do was watch as his brother stalked back inside the bar. All these months, Solomon had believed Kane was locked within himself, dealing with his own demons. Meanwhile, Kane had been assessing everyone and everything.

Solomon raked a hand through his hair. He would have to keep an eye on Kane. Still waters ran deep, and Kane's were as still as glass.

He pivoted and made his way to the stairs. Every step that brought him closer to Minka tightened the knot of anxiety and anticipation within him. He honestly couldn't decide which emotion he felt more. And that made everything worse.

His hand hovered over the keypad before he punched in the code and heard the locks shift. He opened the door to the sound of jazz music. Slipping inside, he quietly shut the metal slab behind him.

A quick glance around the studio found Minka in the kitchen, moving with the beat of the music as she stirred something in a bowl. On the island behind her were a dozen cupcakes sitting out to cool.

She turned around and began to spread icing on the small treats. Solomon remained immobile as he watched her top each of the cupcakes before she stepped back with a smile and looked at them.

The *ding* of a timer had her spinning around to the oven where she took out another tray of cupcakes and set them to cool. He must have made some sound because her gaze jerked to him.

Minka reached over and turned down the volume on her phone then flashed him a smile. "Hi."

"Hi."

"I hope you don't mind. It's not easy to cook for just one, and after smelling all that delicious food today, I had the need to be in the kitchen."

He walked to the island and looked at the confections. "Of course, I don't mind. And you know these won't last very long."

"I, ah, thought I might cook you dinner."

He held her pale brown eyes and saw the nervousness she couldn't quite hide. Along with the spot of flour on her cheek. "You don't need to do that."

"I'd like to."

"Then I accept." Though he wasn't sure just what he'd given in to. For some reason, it felt like much more than just food.

Her face lit up with a smile. "Great. I hope you like pasta."

"I love it."

She rocked back on her heels and glanced at the floor. "Good. That's good."

The silence that followed grew awkward. Solomon tried

to think of something else to say, but he couldn't think of anything. Finally, he moved to go around Minka the same time she reached for an oven mitt on the island.

They bumped into each other. He instantly grabbed hold of her when she bounced off him so she didn't fall backward. A long, dark curl fell over one eye.

He reached up and smoothed it aside. Then he ran his thumb over the spot of flour, wiping it from her cheek. The contact of his skin against hers did strange, wonderful things to him.

It reminded him of having her close to him in the shower. What a fool he'd been to argue with her instead of drawing her close and tasting those full lips of hers. The water had soaked her clothes, but he'd been too incensed to pay attention as he should have.

That was his loss to be sure. One he wouldn't repeat—if he had the chance again.

"Flour," he murmured.

She blinked, nodding absently as their gazes remained locked. "It gets everywhere."

"Yes." He slowly brushed the tip of her nose and then her collarbone. "Everywhere."

The awkward silence shifted to one filled with sexual tension. As much as he wanted to kiss her, he couldn't. He needed to keep his mind focused on Delphine and the impending attack.

To give in to the need pounding through him, the hunger

that threatened to bring him to his knees would only cloud his thoughts. Instead of keeping Minka safe, he could be putting her in more danger if he didn't remain focused.

He dropped his arms to his sides and took a step back. It was one of the hardest things he'd ever done, but he was doing it for her. For if she died because of him, he wouldn't be able to live with the consequences.

"I think I'm going to take a shower and wash off the smell of the kitchen." He turned his lips up into a smile and walked around her.

He fought not to look back at her as he made his way into the bathroom and pulled the door closed. Standing in the middle of the room with his hands clenched at his sides and his eyes closed, Solomon tried to bring his body back under control. All he wanted to do was go back out there and pull her against him, to thread his fingers in her curls and hold her head steady as he ravaged her lips.

Blowing out a ragged breath, he opened his eyes and turned on the shower. He stripped and tossed his clothes into the hamper.

When he opened the glass door of the enclosure, he pictured Minka standing there as she had earlier that morning. Her eyes had blazed with fury, making them sparkle. She'd been indignant, outraged.

And it had turned him on.

He stepped beneath the spray and quickly shut off the hot water. The frigid spray did little to cool his body. Not when

Minka filled his home, mind, and his senses.

It had been easy to be around her while she slept. Now that she was awake, she was an enticement he couldn't ignore. A temptation he craved.

How in the hell was he going to survive the next few days? He snorted. Days? It could be weeks. There was no way he was strong enough to withstand her. Every minute she was near, it was becoming harder and harder for him to remember why he wanted to keep her at arm's length.

After all, Myles was right. Minka was strong. Physically, mentally, and magically. She was everything Misty hadn't been. That in and of itself gave Minka a fighting chance to survive whatever was coming their way.

Then an image of Misty lying dead in the street, her arm outstretched toward him, flashed in Solomon's mind. And just like that, all the yearning he'd felt for Minka vanished.

It was better that way.

For everyone.

Chapter 9

LAWS OF ATTRACTION HAD A WAY OF PUTTING THINGS out of reach. Just when Minka thought there might be something between her and Solomon, she was reminded yet again of the gulf that divided them.

It didn't matter how attracted she was to him because there was something that kept him from showing her the same. That meant it was in her best interest to leave things alone and forget about Solomon LaRue once and for all.

If only it were that easy.

She shook her head and set about washing the pans she'd dirtied while making the cupcakes. While wiping the island and counters clean, she heard the shower cut off.

Minka turned to dump the crumbs into the sink when everything faded. There was never any warning when the visions occurred, but more troubling was the fact that she was having another so soon after the previous one.

She tried to grab hold of something, anything as she felt

herself falling, but her body wouldn't listen. As the world around her wilted away to be replaced with another, the first thing she heard was the laughter.

There was no reason for her to look for the source. It was a voice she recognized. Delphine. That maniacal laughter sent chills of dread down her spine.

"It's all your fault, Minka."

Delphine's voice was all around her. Minka turned to discover she was in the middle of the street outside of Gator Bait. There were so many dead bodies—humans, djinn, vampires, witches, and werewolves—that she had to pick and choose where she stepped.

Yet there was no sign of Delphine.

But the crazy bitch was there. Minka could feel her.

"Look at what you've done," Delphine said. "Look!"

Minka gravitated toward the platinum fur of a werewolf. She knew it was Solomon, but the sight of his snowy fur tinged with red made her turn her head away.

"What do you want?" Minka shouted into the air, her head turning this way and that searching for Delphine.

Movement out of the corner of her eye had her spinning around. The sight of Delphine covered in blood made Minka take a step back.

Delphine continued toward her, walking on the bodies as if they were steppingstones. She didn't stop until she stood before Minka. "You want to know what I want? It's you, witch. You're what I want."

"Why?"

"You can save the innocents. You can even save your friends," Delphine continued, her arm sweeping from left to right to encompass everyone.

Minka glanced down at Solomon's dead body. "What do I need to do?"

"Surrender to me."

"And if I don't?"

"What you see here is just the beginning if you fight me."

Minka swallowed hard. "This isn't a vision, is it?"

"Sort of." Delphine smiled. "You've had this vision before. I thought it fitting to use for me to talk to you."

"You could've called."

Delphine chuckled. "Oh, I do like your spirit, Minka. But you and I both know this is the only way."

Minka knew the priestess was powerful, but she hadn't realized Delphine was able to enter someone's visions. That was...troubling.

"You have twenty-four hours to come to me. Else, you've sealed everyone's fate," Delphine stated.

And just like that, the vision and talk with Delphine ended. Thankfully. Minka blinked and found herself looking up at Solomon, who was wearing a concerned frown. It was then she realized she was on the floor as he held her upper body, and she clung to his shirtless shoulders as if he were all that was keeping her alive.

His hand smoothed back her curls. "How bad was it?"

The impact of Delphine's words hit her like a wrecking ball. She kept seeing Solomon's dead body in her mind's eye.

"Breathe," he urged her.

She nodded, only then noticing that she was close to hyperventilating.

He didn't ask anything more, simply brought her against his chest and held her, rocking slowly back and forth. His hard muscles, warm skin, and secure hold were just what she needed. As the minutes ticked by, she found herself calming. Yet he continued to hold her, and it was the greatest feeling in the world.

"I'm scared," she admitted.

He rested his chin atop her head. "I'd be worried if you weren't."

"I think we've underestimated Delphine."

There was a pause before he asked, "How?"

"She caused this vision. It was a repeat of the one I had at my house. Except this time, she put herself there in order to talk to me." When Solomon didn't reply, Minka leaned back to look at him. "She said it was the only way she could tell me her offer."

Blue eyes narrowed as anger sparked. "What offer?"

"She said the slaughter I saw in my vision will happen if I fight her."

"No," Solomon stated with a shake of his head.

Unable to hold his gaze, she looked away. "Delphine said if I come to her in the next twenty-four hours, all of you will live."

"No," he said again, this time more firmly.

His finger on her chin turned her head toward him. Their gazes clashed, locked. Water dripped from the ends of his hair onto his chest before it made its way down his stomach.

She took a deep breath. "I could save all of you."

"It's a trap."

"What if it isn't?"

His face contorted with frustration and anger. "You can't really be taking her offer seriously."

"You didn't see what I did. I stood over your body, Solomon." Minka pushed out of his arms and climbed to her feet.

He was quick to stand. "If she can get into your head to talk to you, did it never occur to you to think that she could also *give* you that vision?"

"I...." She threw up her arms in defeat. "I don't know. It's a possibility, I suppose."

"Damn right, it is."

"What if it's not? What if my vision is real?"

His chest heaved as he pressed his lips together. "You can't go to her."

"I can't be responsible for those deaths. Your death."

His hands came up on either side of her face. "You won't be."

"I will!"

"I won't let it happen."

His words barely registered before his mouth was on hers. As soon as their lips touched, they both stilled. She leaned back and looked at him. The blatant desire she saw in his blue eyes sent her heart careening in her chest.

She wrapped her arms around his neck and kissed him. This time, he held her tightly and moved his lips over hers. As soon as she parted her mouth, his tongue slipped inside to dance with hers.

The moan that rumbled in his chest made her stomach quiver with desire. Then he tilted his head and deepened the kiss. She felt his arousal through the towel. It sent heat and need barreling through her.

She ripped off his towel and ran her hands over his hard, muscular physique. Scars littered his body, reminding her of how often he put his life on the line. He might be a werewolf, but he wasn't immortal.

Their passionate kisses paused only long enough for her to remove her shirt. The fire within her blazed hotly, the hunger consuming her.

He unclasped her bra as he walked her backward. Minka discarded the garment and went back to running her palms over his amazing body right up until her legs hit the back of the bed.

She toppled backward and rose up on her elbows to look at him. "Magnificent," she murmured.

"Yes, you are," he said as he leaned down and unbuttoned her jeans.

Then he grabbed the hems at her ankles and jerked the denim off with one yank. His blue eyes flashed yellow, a sign of the wolf within. Her breath locked in her throat—she was so turned on. He said not a word as he reached down and grabbed the waist of her lace panties before ripping them in half.

She lay back on the bed as he tossed aside the ruined garment. A smile curled her lips when he crawled over. Her hands found his hips before moving to his ass.

Skin to skin, body to body. Could anything be more decadent or intimate? He kissed her slowly, lazily, as if he had all the time in the world and wanted to savor every second.

It was erotic and stimulating. And she wanted more.

His mouth traveled down her neck before returning to hers for more of their fiery kisses. His hands were everywhere, softly caressing, pressing, and simply holding.

"God, I need you," he rasped in her ear.

She arched her back, offering herself. "I'm yours."

As if her words had unlocked whatever was holding him back, he groaned loudly and skimmed his hand up her side until he reached her breast.

She held her breath, waiting for him to touch her. He moved his hand gradually upward until he cupped her breast and gently massaged the orb.

Her breath rushed past her lips as her eyes slid shut. The feel of his large, calloused hand on her was heavenly. He knew just where to touch, just how to tease her to the point of pain.

He tweaked her nipple before skimming his palm over the aching tips. Then he rolled the nipple between his fingers, lightly pinching the peak.

Her breasts swelled from the attention. All the while, her hips bucked against him, wanting and needing the friction the movement caused.

"So damn beautiful," he murmured.

She gasped when his mouth locked onto a nipple and began to suckle while his fingers teased her other peak mercilessly. The assault on her breasts stole her breath and flooded her body with such desire that she shook with the force of it.

Her fingers dug into his arms as she moaned. He rocked forward, his arousal rubbing against her swollen clit. She sucked in a breath at the contact.

"I need you inside me," she told him as she opened her eyes. "I want to feel you."

He lifted his head and smiled. "Not yet."

She started to beg when his finger circled her clit. All thoughts vanished as her body shuddered and her legs fell open. Cool air hit her heated sex. The sight of him looking down at her exposed body brought another rush of warmth.

"I'm going to feast on this," he told her without looking up from her sex.

Minka couldn't take her eyes from him as he settled between her legs. He glanced up at her right before his mouth lowered to her core.

His tongue gently lapped at the juncture of her thighs. First one side, then the other. He softly blew against her heated flesh before he leaned down and circled her clit with his tongue.

The pleasure that jolted through her was intense and blinding. A cry left her lips when his tongue began to move back and forth over the tiny nub in quick strokes.

Just as he'd said he would, he feasted upon her sex. Each lick of his tongue sent her higher, her desire swelling until she was crazed with it.

Until she was crying out for him to give her the release she craved.

Then he slid a finger inside her.

Chapter 10

PERFECTION. THAT'S WHAT SOLOMON THOUGHT OF Minka. From her mocha-colored skin to her pale brown eyes to her curly hair.

He couldn't stop touching her silky flesh. Her body was soft and lithe, and so damn responsive. Her breasts fit in the palms of his hands while her dark nipples remained hard and ultra-sensitive.

Yet it was her hot, wet center that occupied his attention at the moment. Dark curls tried to hide her sex from him. He spread her woman's lips and licked her clit until she was a writhing, incoherent mess.

Only then did he thrust a finger into her tight body. He ran his free hand along her outer thigh. Her cries were music to his ears and pushed him to bring her higher. What a fool he'd been to try and resist the attraction, the overwhelming hunger to unite their bodies.

He added a second finger to the first as he thrust slowly

and deeply. Her hips were lifting to meet his hand while her chest rose and fell rapidly.

Watching her reaction to his teasing of her body was mesmerizing. He could do it all day, and still never get enough. Not in a month. Not in a lifetime.

His cock jumped when he circled her clit with his thumb, and her back arched off the bed. He couldn't wait to be inside her, to feel the hot walls of her sex hold him, to move within her and feel her wet heat surrounding him.

He knew the moment her climax hit by the way her body stiffened and her breath hitched. His gaze was locked on her face as the pleasure stole over her features and softened her lips into an O.

There had never been a more beautiful sight than Minka in the throws of an orgasm. It was an image that would be with him until the day his heart stopped beating.

He withdrew his hand from her sex and spread his palm over her belly. Her eyes fluttered open with her lips curving into a seductive smile.

"I need you inside me," she said.

As if he could deny her now. In truth, there wasn't anything he would refuse her. He'd known Minka was extraordinary, that she would consume him—body and soul. It was why he'd tried to be mean to her in order for her to hate him. Because he'd known he couldn't resist her forever.

He rose up over her, his hands on either side of her head. Pale brown eyes gazed up at him, sparking with a fiery passion that made his balls tighten.

Without a word, she rolled onto her stomach and looked back at him over her shoulder. Her sexy grin made him groan as he ran a hand down her spine to her round ass.

When she rose up on all fours and rocked back, grinding into his hard cock, he got on his knees and clasped his hands on her hips to hold her still. She fell forward onto her elbows, her head down, waiting. Then he guided himself into her entrance.

The moment he pushed inside her, she sucked in a breath. He slowly filled her inch by inch. The feeling of her surrounding him like a glove brought him to the edge. It was only by sheer will alone that he held back his climax.

With one final push, he was fully seated within her. For several seconds, neither of them moved. He brushed aside her long curls and caressed a hand down her back.

He began to move, slowly at first to draw out their lovemaking. But the tempo soon quickened as passion wrapped around them tightly.

Minka came up on her hands, rocking back to meet each of his thrusts. He reached for her face, turning her head to the side to see her. His chest tightened when he saw that her lips were parted and her eyes were closed. But it was the pleasure he witnessed in every detail of her face that broke through the last shreds of his control.

He pounded into her as he lifted her upper body to his. There, he ran his hands over her breasts, tweaking her nipples as he brought them closer and closer to the bliss that waited.

She reached a hand back, wrapping it around his head as she twisted to put her lips on his. Their tongues danced in time with the movement of their bodies, tightening the bonds that were tethering them together.

He didn't even care. All that mattered was the yearning, the craving he had for the amazing woman in his arms.

"Solomon," she murmured between kisses.

Her hands were rubbing along his sides, down his thighs, and over his hands that caressed her body. Never had he experienced anything so sensual, so carnal.

She fell forward onto her hands again when he stroked her clit once more. With just a few swipes of his finger, she threw back her head and cried out as a second orgasm ripped through her.

He was so unprepared for the feeling of her body clamping around him that it tipped him over the edge. He welcomed the climax, embraced the rampant ecstasy that devoured him. It grabbed hold of him, consuming every fiber of his being until he felt his heart beating with Minka's.

Only then did he open his eyes as the last of the orgasm faded. And he realized he was a new man: a man who had tasted the pleasure of the woman who was his other half.

And he knew now that he would do absolutely anything to keep her safe and alive. Because she was his life, his very reason for breathing.

Solomon leaned over her and wrapped his arms around

her as she struggled to get her breathing back to normal. He rolled to his side, taking her with him. He moved aside her hair and kissed her cheek.

"Why did we wait so long to do that?" she asked.

He put his lips against her neck and grinned. "Because I'm an idiot."

She laughed and turned her head to him, their eyes meeting. "I feel you inside me."

"It's where I always want to be."

"It's where I want you to be."

He skimmed his fingers down her face. "I don't know what just happened between us, but I've never felt anything like that before. It's almost as if...."

"It was destined," she finished.

"Yes."

She sighed and turned her head back to face front. Then she put her arms over his. "It's too bad we can't stay right here forever."

"What you said earlier about Delphine..." he began.

"Please, don't," she interrupted him. "I don't want to talk about her."

He pulled out of her and leaned up on an elbow to look down at her. "I do. Because I refuse to let you go to that nutjob as a sacrifice."

Her head turned to him. A sad smile pulled at her lips as she touched his face. "And I'll gladly do it to save you and the others. I can't have your blood on my hands."

"Who says you will?"

"My visions come true."

He twisted his lips. "Yes. And no. You saw Myles die, but you didn't see yourself pulling the silver from his body and saving his life."

She flattened her lips, refusing to reply.

"Admit it," he urged. "Your visions show you only part of a scenario."

"Of course, they do."

"And our decisions can change the course."

She shifted to face him, coming up on an elbow so they were face-to-face. "As long as I've had my visions, there's only been one who has changed what I've seen. Myles."

"Don't you want to try?"

"Yes," she insisted.

He took her hand in his. "Then stand with me, with us. Don't give Delphine what she wants."

"You're asking the impossible."

"No. I'm asking you to trust me."

Her face crumpled. "I do. I always have. But I saw you. Dead. Your ashy white fur covered in blood. That image haunts me. I can't have it happen."

He pulled her against him then. They clung to each other, each lost in their own thoughts. Solomon couldn't lose her. Not now. Not ever. He'd already suffered one unbearable loss, and he wasn't strong enough to endure another.

More than that, he knew in his gut that Delphine was

tricking Minka. But how to convince her of that? She was sure her vision was real. Though he hated to admit it, he'd go to extremes to make sure his family and friends were spared a horrific death.

So he couldn't fault Minka there. But that didn't mean he'd stand aside and let her go to Delphine. If she wouldn't fight for herself, then he'd do it for her.

No matter what the Voodoo priestess told Minka, eventually, Delphine would come for all of them. She only spared someone if she thought she could give them more pain later on. It was how Delphine always worked.

Minka might have grown up in New Orleans, but her coven had kept its distance from Delphine. Solomon and his family hadn't had that luxury. They'd been front and center in numerous altercations with the priestess. Delphine was the cause of his parents' deaths, and she'd already made it clear she wanted Riley for something.

The LaRues and Chiassons readily gave their blood and their lives to protect the innocent. It was a family tradition, one that Solomon had never thought twice about.

Until now.

Minka made him long for a normal life. One where he worried about paying bills and his main concern was pleasing Minka. But longing for such a life didn't make it so.

He was a LaRue, a werewolf that policed the paranormal factions of New Orleans to keep everyone in line. Delphine's rise to power had been done with fear and murder. His parents had tried to stop her, and look where it had gotten them.

It was why he and his brothers had trodden carefully with the priestess. And what had led them to the current situation.

They should've taken Delphine down as soon as they could. The problem was, he wasn't certain she could be killed. Her power frightened him because it seemed far-reaching.

Everyone in the city feared her, whether they knew her or not. That kind of terror couldn't be erased easily. It had taken years to seep into everyone's subconscious, causing everyone to do exactly as Delphine wanted.

Well, Solomon wouldn't be one of those puppets anymore.

It might end up costing him his life, but it might end up freeing others. He was ashamed that he'd taken so long to come to such a decision.

Yet every time he thought of Delphine, it was the image of his parents lying dead in the street, their bloodied hands joined, and Delphine looking on with a smile that he saw.

All these years, he'd thought he'd been handling the priestess carefully but with authority. When, in fact, she'd been the one handling him. It infuriated Solomon. That, combined with the fact that he'd been blind to it all, made him silently rage.

Delphine's time ruling New Orleans was over. If they didn't stop her now, she might very well be unstoppable. That would leave nothing but grief to any and all who came to the city.

He took one of Minka's curls and wrapped it around his finger. His heart ached for time with her. To learn what she loved and hated, to find her favorite food, to discover what flowers she liked.

He wanted to take her to the movies, to share a bottle of wine, and to sit silently as they watched a lightning storm over the river.

He wanted to grumble about her stuff cluttering his bathroom and go furniture shopping with her.

He yearned to hold her hand as they walked down the street, to pick out a Christmas tree with her, and to have her beside him at the table for Thanksgiving.

He craved to have her with him as they climbed into bed at night, and wake holding her each morning.

And he knew what all of that meant, what he'd known for months and wouldn't admit...he was in love with Minka Verdin.

Chapter 11

Minka had never known such happiness. She licked the sauce from her fingers and stirred the mixture in the pan atop the stove. She looked over at Solomon, who was shredding fresh parmesan for her.

He met her gaze and grinned. "That shirt looks damn good on you."

She chuckled and looked down at his shirt that she'd put on. The denim button-down hit her upper thighs, and she'd had to roll up the sleeves in order to cook, but having his scent on her and wearing his shirt made her feel...like they were a couple.

Though she wasn't sure what they were exactly. Neither had spoken about it. And really, why? If she were going to Delphine, there was no need to go into a lengthy discussion on what they were or weren't.

No more had been said about Delphine or Minka's visions since Solomon had brought it up earlier, and Minka was just fine with that.

"That smells delicious," Solomon said as he came to stand behind her.

She leaned back against him when he put his hands on her waist. Stirring the creamy sauce, she added more cayenne pepper to the mix. "It's my grandmother's recipe."

"How much longer? My mouth is watering."

Laughing, she reached over and stirred the pot of boiling pasta. "Not long now."

"Good. How about some wine?"

"Yes, please."

Her gaze followed as Solomon moved away to the nice stock of wine he had. Everything seemed so normal at the moment, and she wanted to soak up every second of it. Her twenty-four hours was rapidly counting down.

While he opened the bottle of chardonnay, Minka added the shrimp to the sauce to cook the last few minutes before the pasta was finished.

Solomon turned on some background music. She smiled, wishing they had more time together. He was an amazing lover, both tender and demanding. With him, she felt special and beautiful, and she knew how unique something like that was. If there were a way for her to fight Delphine and keep Solomon and the others alive, she'd do it in a heartbeat.

But the vision had shown her exactly what would happen.

She drained the pasta and added it in with the shrimp and sauce, stirring it all together. Then she dumped in the parmesan and mixed it again. By the time she finished, Solomon had the two plates out, waiting.

He bent over and drew in a deep breath of the dish. "Damn. My mouth is watering. You'd better put some on my plate before I take the pot from you and eat it all."

She laughed and gave him a heaping portion before dishing some onto her plate. Then she joined him at the island where the wine was waiting for them.

Solomon lifted his wine glass. "Here's to the future."

"The future," she replied and clinked their glasses together.

She held his gaze as they both took a drink. The toast could be taken various ways, but she knew Solomon was thinking about her staying to fight against Delphine.

But she forgot all of that when he lifted his fork and brought a bite to his lips. His eyes closed and his face filled with delight as he chewed.

When he swallowed, he looked at her. "This needs to go on our menu. It's that good."

"I'm glad you like it." In fact, she was beaming inside.

The conversation remained light and flowed freely as they ate. They spoke of the bar, his brothers, and Court and Skye's wedding that everyone was expecting.

All too soon, their plates were cleaned, and the wine bottle was empty. She rose to take the dishes to the sink when Solomon took her hand.

"I'll do that later," he said. "Come with me."

She allowed him to pull her after him as he rose and walked

to the sofa. With a click of a remote, the lights shut off, and she was able to look out the wall of windows to the Quarter.

"This is beautiful."

He pulled her down beside him and leaned back. "It's one of my favorite things about this place."

"It's magical. That's for sure."

Her eyes briefly closed when his fingers tugged on the ends of her hair. She turned to face him before crawling to straddle his waist.

"I wish I knew a spell to stop time," she said.

His hands came to rest on her hips before sliding beneath the hem of her shirt. "Maybe we can will it to happen if we both wish it hard enough."

"If only it were that simple."

"All these months, we could've been together." His forehead creased as he shook his head in agitation.

Minka ran her thumb over his bottom lip. "Don't look at the past. We only have the present. Let's make the most of it."

She slid her hands into his blond hair before leaning down to kiss him. His hands flattened on her back and pressed her closer as he deepened the embrace.

Desire that had been banked blazed between them. Minka began unbuttoning her shirt before Solomon grew impatient and yanked it open, the buttons flying around them to ping softly on the wooden floor.

Delphine stared at the darkened windows of Solomon LaRue's loft. She'd hoped to get Minka before the witch and the werewolf slept together, but she'd waited just a little too long.

That changed very little in her plan. She wasn't giving Minka any time to form a strong attachment to Solomon. In the end, Minka would come to her to save her friends.

The smell of bayou and werewolf assaulted her. Delphine turned her head to the shadows and motioned her visitor forward. "I don't like when you skulk, Griffin."

"I warned you about Solomon's attraction to her."

Delphine waved away his words with a flutter of her fingers. "Tell me, how long was she with Solomon before you came to me?"

"What does that matter? I told you where she was."

"Ah. So you did." She turned to face him, letting her gaze rake over his face.

His green eyes briefly met hers before looking back at Solomon's windows.

"When did Minka arrive in the city, Griffin?"

"A few days ago," he said with a shrug.

Anger flashed through her. With merely a thought, she had him pinned against the building. She curled her fingers into a fist. That gesture was enough to squeeze his throat, choking him.

He clawed at the invisible fingers at his neck, his eyes

bulging.

"If you'd come to me as soon as they brought her to the city, I could've prevented her and Solomon's union," she told Griffin.

She wanted to end Griffin's life right then, but unfortunately, she needed him for the next part of her plan. With a roll of her eyes, she released him. He bent over at the waist, gulping in huge mouthfuls of air.

"You care about Minka," Delphine said. "But who do you want to save? The witch? Or your sister?"

Griffin's eyes flashed yellow in his anger as he straightened. "I'm doing all of this for Elin. You promised to release her in exchange for my knowledge."

"So I did. That directive didn't mean for you to wait days before sharing information with me. It makes me think you're regretting our partnership."

He gave a loud snort. "A partnership implies we have the same goal. You want Minka and the LaRues. I just want my sister."

"How is the rest of your pack going to feel when they learn you helped to wipe out the LaRues?" she asked with a smile.

Griffin glanced away. "They won't know."

She took a step toward him. "And why not? Nothing in our agreement said I couldn't tell anyone I wanted that you're helping me bring down the LaRues." She tsked. "After all that work you did to get Kane to trust you and bring you into the fold with his brothers... That gave you the opportunity to call back all the Moonstone weres, who had scattered to the wind after your parents betrayed Solomon's. I suppose the apple really doesn't fall too far from the tree."

"You have my sister!" Griffin shouted.

Delphine raised a brow and narrowed her gaze. "Keep your voice down, wolf, or I'll take it from you."

He took a few steps away, running a hand down his face before he walked back to her. "All I want is my sister back."

"That's not true. You want your pack to be allowed to remain in New Orleans."

The frown that formed on his face nearly made her laugh. How easy it was to manipulate all the pathetic creatures— human and paranormal alike.

"You said we could remain, unharmed by you," Griffin replied in a low, angry voice.

"What I said was that you and your sister would be allowed to stay. Everyone else in your pack I'm going to hunt and kill, slowly," she said with a smile.

He shook his head and gave her a disgruntled look. "Why? I've done everything you wanted."

"And you'll continue to be a good watchdog, or I'll kill Elin." She laughed when he looked confused and frustrated. "Did you really think you could try and make a deal with me? As soon as I took your sister, I knew you'd do whatever I wanted, whenever I wanted."

Griffin's chest heaved in fury as he glared at her. "You're a cold bitch, Delphine."

"I want power, and I know what to do to get it."

"Yeah," Griffin turned on his heel and stalked into the night.

Delphine watched him go before she looked to one of her disciples who always followed. She gave a jerk of her chin that sent the man following Griffin.

Holding Elin should keep the Alpha in line, but just in case it didn't, she was going to have him followed. It would be just like the whimpering werewolf to have a conscience and go see Solomon. Or worse, Minka.

One time, before the weres had risen up against her, she'd squashed that rebellion easily enough by threatening Griffin's life. That's all it had taken to get his parents to do exactly what she wanted.

For years, the only werewolves she'd had to worry about were the LaRues. Neither the LaRues nor the Moonstone pack was aware of how close they'd come to killing her when they attacked her to free Minka and Addison.

It was why she was going to rid New Orleans of every werewolf and ensure that none ever ventured near the city again. To help her cause, she would put a bounty on any werewolf. Whoever killed one and brought her the carcass would get payment—either in money or erasure of debt.

Because everyone was indebted to her in one form or another.

She'd spent her life getting to this point, and she wasn't going to have it fall apart because one witch decided to stand up against her.

Yet it wasn't just Minka refusing to come to her. Delphine had seen it all in her own vision. If Minka stood with Solomon and the LaRues, it would unite the entire Moonstone pack. That would then be the end of her.

It was why she'd taken Elin years ago. Insurance. And Elin would be the sole reason Delphine got Minka's power, the LaRues would be wiped out, and the Moonstone pack would be hunted to extinction.

Chapter 12

MINKA STOOD IN THE MIDDLE OF SOLOMON'S LOFT AND looked around. They'd made love on every surface, in every way throughout the night.

She was tired, but her body had never been so pleasured. And never would be again.

Her gaze went to the bed. It was a blessing that she'd woken to find him gone. It gave her the time she needed to get dressed and gather her few belongings without him attempting to convince her to stay.

She didn't know what Delphine had planned for her. Most likely, it was death, but that was preferable to having her friends die in her stead.

Minka grabbed her bag and walked to the door. As she stepped outside, she looked within one last time. She'd been amazingly happy there for the short time she'd had.

Closing the door behind her, she started down the steps, only to come to a halt when she spotted Solomon standing at the bottom as he leaned a shoulder against the building.

"I thought you were gone," she said.

"I've been waiting for you."

She frowned as she slowly descended the steps. "And you couldn't do that in your place?"

"Not when I needed backup."

"Backup?"

He nodded and took her bag when she reached him. Then he put his hand on her back and guided her through the kitchen door into Gator Bait. There, everyone stood—even Griffin.

She looked around at all the faces before she turned to Solomon. "What is this?"

"An intervention," Riley said.

Minka shot Solomon a stern look before she faced the others. "Thank you for this, but it isn't going to work. None of you saw my vision. You don't know what it's like to see all of you dead. I can stop that from happening."

"By going to that bitch?" Kane asked with a snort. "You're smarter than that, Minka."

And this was why she hadn't wanted to tell anyone her plan. "I'm trying to save all of you."

Solomon came up beside her and took her hand. "It won't work. Even if you go to her, Delphine will come for all of us. She sees us as a threat."

"She promised to leave each of you alone," Minka insisted.

Myles said, "She lies to get what she wants. Look at the

extremes she went to in order to capture you and Addison?"

"He's right," Addison interjected. "Delphine can't be trusted."

Skye's dark eyes were filled with anxiousness. "You helped save me not so long ago. Let us help you now."

"We're rather good at it," Court added.

Everyone had spoken except for Griffin. Minka thought that odd since he'd been so vocal while watching over her at the plantation. Why was he so silent now?

"I've got an idea," Solomon said, breaking into her thoughts. "Hear me out before you leave."

There was still time, but she knew every second she remained with Solomon, the harder it would be to leave him. Yet she couldn't walk away without listening to him.

His bright blue eyes held hers, silently waiting. She gave a nod, and he rubbed his thumb along the back of her hand.

After he sat her bag down near the back door, they followed the others into the front of the bar. It was odd to see it so empty and quiet. Almost as if the place were waiting to come to life with people and music again.

Minka took the chair Solomon pulled out for her and found herself sitting between him and Kane. Others dragged up chairs, except for Griffin, who half-sat on one of the tables.

"Please reconsider your decision," Addison implored, her hazel eyes pleading.

Riley crossed one long leg over the other and tossed her long, brunette locks over her shoulder. "In your place, I'd probably do exactly the same, Minka. But the thing is, it's the wrong choice."

"What are Delphine's plans for you?" Kane asked.

Minka hesitated before she shrugged. "I'm not sure. I assume she plans to finish what she began with Addison and me."

"Which means she'll come for Addison again," Myles stated in a harsh voice. "I didn't let Delphine kill Addison the first time, and I won't this time either."

Minka shifted in her chair. "Delphine hasn't said anything about wanting Addison. Our agreement was that she would leave all of you alone if I came to her in the allotted time."

"And you believe her?" Skye asked.

Minka shrugged. "No, but I don't have another choice."

"You do," Solomon said and reached over to take her hand. "Stand and fight with us. We've proven what we can do together."

"If I do that, all of you die."

Kane leaned his arms on the table. "You're a powerful witch. It stands to reason that Delphine would want you out of the way. If you really believe that all of us will be alive years from now because Delphine held up her end of the bargain, then I'll take you to her myself."

"I see the doubt in your eyes," Solomon told her. "You know as well as I that Delphine will come for us. We're a threat to her. She wants us out of the way."

Riley nodded slowly. "And the first step is you."

Minka didn't want to die. She also didn't want to hand over her magic in any form to anyone, much less Delphine. But she wanted to save her friends more than anything. Were they right? Was she just handing herself over to Delphine, which would clear the way for the priestess to kill the others?

That thought left her cold.

"What if all of you are wrong? What if my vision comes true?" she asked.

Solomon brought her hand to his lips and kissed her knuckles. "Then we'll have died fighting against evil as we were meant to do."

"What about you, Griffin?" Court asked.

All eyes swung to the Alpha of the Moonstone pack. He had one hand by his lips. He dropped his arm and shrugged. "It's always been the duty of my pack to protect the LaRues and to fight beside you."

Court's gaze narrowed on him. "That's true enough, but the past speaks for itself."

"I'm not my parents," Griffin declared.

Minka frowned as she watched Griffin. There was something off about him. As if he were nervous and his mind was elsewhere, which was decidedly odd since this involved his pack.

"What?" Solomon leaned over and whispered.

She shrugged, unable to pinpoint the problem. But, obviously, she wasn't the only one. Court had seen something, as well. Why else was he directing such questions toward

Griffin?

"You were adamant about protecting Minka in the bayou," Solomon said to Griffin. "In fact, we came to blows over it. I get the impression your thoughts have changed."

Griffin got to his feet. "I vowed to protect Minka."

"What of your sister? Delphine still holds Elin," Kane said.

The longer Minka watched Griffin, the more she was sure that he was somehow involved with Delphine. She didn't want to come out and accuse him of it in case she was wrong, and she also didn't want him to know anything more about her decision. In fact, she had a plan of her own.

"I'm going to Delphine," she declared.

There was a moment of silence, then Myles asked, "We can't change your mind?"

"No," she said and glanced at Griffin.

Solomon jumped to his feet and stood with his hands fisted at his sides while glaring at her. "I sure the hell can. I'll tie you to my bed if I have to."

She calmly stood and put her hand on his chest while she held his gaze. After a moment, Solomon blew out a breath and stalked to the back of the bar.

While the others began talking at once, there were two who remained silent. Kane, who watched her with narrowed eyes, and Griffin, who kept looking out the windows.

That was all the answer she needed. Minka held up her hand for the others to quiet. Then she looked at each of them. "I'd like to take a few minutes with each of you to say goodbye."

"Minka—" Skye began, but Court quickly grabbed her hand to silence her.

Minka walked to Griffin and smiled up at him. "Thank you for watching over me these last months. You were a welcome diversion. I treasured the time I had to get to know you."

A muscle jumped in Griffin's jaw as he frowned. She squeezed his hands and then stepped back. Without a word, he pivoted and walked out the back door.

As soon as the door had closed behind him, Minka blew out a breath. Her gaze landed on Solomon, who stood at the doorway to the kitchen, staring at her. He made his way to her, cupping her face in his hands and giving her a soft kiss.

"What was that about?" he asked.

Court propped a foot on a chair. "She saw what I did. Griffin is working with Delphine."

"He wouldn't," Kane protested.

Myles ran a hand down his face. "I'm inclined to agree with the others, Kane. Something was off about him."

"Not to mention that Delphine has his sister," Riley pointed out.

Minka linked her hand with Solomon's and faced the group. "This isn't Griffin's fault. I'm sure Delphine is using Elin against him."

"To do what?" Skye asked.

Minka shrugged, her lips twisting. "Probably to report on me."

"Are you really going to Delphine?" Addison asked.

She shook her head and felt Solomon's grip on her tighten. "It was a ploy to get Griffin to leave so we could talk freely."

"The fight is on," Riley said and slammed her hands on the table with a bright smile. "I've been waiting for this."

Solomon held up a hand. "Hold on. Things just got more complicated. My plan relied on the Moonstone pack for help. Without them...well, I don't need to tell you that that puts us at a distinct disadvantage."

"Perhaps not totally," Kane said.

Myles lifted a shoulder. "All right. I'll bite. What does that mean?"

"It means that I might be able to bring the Moonstone pack here," Kane explained.

Riley's smile died and a frown formed. "If Griffin finds out, he'll consider that a challenge. Y'all will fight to the death."

"I know."

Minka looked at Solomon, who was staring at Kane silently. She moved closer to Solomon. "We're going to need all the help we can get besides the werewolves. The djinn and vampires won't ever unite to stand against Delphine, but there are witches who will."

"I'll come with you," Addison said.

"Whoa. Hold up," Solomon said. "Minka isn't leaving the building. As soon as Delphine realizes she has lied, the priestess will be coming for Minka and all of us."

Kane got to his feet. "Which means we have no time to

lose."

"Wait," Minka said, stopping everyone. "Delphine has this place watched. If any of us leave, we'll be tracked. She'll know what we're doing before we can do any of it."

Solomon gave a nod of agreement. "Then what do you propose?"

Minka found a smile pulling at her lips as she looked at each of them. They had gathered together to keep her with them, and to let her know how much she was loved.

Now it was time for her to once more make a stand. This time, she knew what was coming. This time, she'd be ready to take on Delphine.

"With magic, of course," she replied.

Chapter 13

Never had so much been on the line. Solomon barely contained his fury over Griffin. It didn't help that Minka excused his behavior. Nor did the fact that Solomon would do the same thing if Delphine held one of his brothers.

He stood off to the side in the bar, his gaze locked on Minka. She'd cleared a section toward a back corner where she sat cross-legged on the floor with her eyes closed and candles surrounding her.

"So," Myles said as he came to stand beside him. "You took my advice."

Solomon slid his gaze to his brother and stared at him before putting his finger to his lips. Then he whispered, "I won't lose her."

"No, you won't," Kane said in a low voice as he came up on Solomon's other side. "I'm going to make sure of that."

Court joined them. "We all are," he mouthed.

Solomon had known his brothers would help, but the

voicing of their conviction alleviated the knot of tension that pressed upon his sternum.

For the next hour, Minka remained in her spot, her lips softly moving. It was growing closer to the time for Gator Bait to open for lunch, and Solomon was getting nervous.

Every person he saw pass by Gator Bait's windows was a potential enemy. Part of him wanted to close the bar, but to do so would give Delphine a win. And right now, he was all about disrupting anything the priestess wanted.

Riley, Skye, and Addison were moving silently about the bar, getting things ready for the lunch crowd while casting furtive glances in Minka's direction.

Finally, Minka opened her eyes. Her head swiveled toward him, but he didn't release his breath until she gave him a smile. Solomon walked to her with his brothers close on his heels.

"Well?" Court asked her.

Solomon shot his brother a hard look. Then he helped Minka to her feet after she'd blown out the candles.

"I sent the messages," she told them. "All we can do now is wait. I have no way of knowing if anyone will come to help."

Myles crossed his arms over his chest. "And if they do, they could be working with Delphine."

"We're damned if we take their help, and we're damned if we don't," Solomon muttered.

Minka put her free hand on his arm. "We're going to have to trust them. Though, I do propose we keep a close watch on everyone."

Kane gave a loud snort. "That's going to be difficult since they'll outnumber us."

"That takes care of the witches, but what about the werewolves?" Court asked.

Solomon frowned when Minka's face wrinkled. "What is it?" he pushed.

"Well, I contacted Jaxon."

Kane's brows shot up in his forehead. "Are you sure that was a good idea?"

"I only told him it was imperative that the LaRues speak to him privately, and that he not tell anyone where he was going," Minka explained.

Solomon smiled at her. "Smart. That leaves it up to us to convince Jaxon to go against Griffin."

"That's not going to be an easy task," Myles stated.

Court shot Myles a flat look. "When is anything ever? I'll head up to the roof and keep a lookout. By the way, when did you tell everyone to come?"

"Today," Minka said.

Solomon sighed and met Minka's gaze. "Then we'd better get ready."

They disbursed around the bar, each doing their part to make sure everything was in order before opening. When the doors were unlocked, Solomon kept Minka in the back with Kane while he remained at the front with Myles and the girls, looking for any witches or werewolves—or any of

Delphine's disciples.

The first few hours were busy with no sign of any enemies or allies. There were many hours until the end of the day, so Solomon wasn't really expecting anyone until the sun went down. Because of that, he was more than surprised when two young witches walked into the bar.

The way Riley greeted them with a smile meant that this wasn't their first time there. After getting their order, Riley walked to him and said, "They've come to say they're joining us."

"Who exactly?" he asked.

Riley looked over her shoulder at the girls. "Those two. I'll tell Minka."

Solomon wasn't going to turn anyone away. The more that joined them, the better. But he knew their real strength would lie with the werewolves. If only Griffin hadn't turned against them.

As the day wore on, more and more witches came into the bar, declaring their intentions to join. By sunset, the LaRues had over thirty witches willing to stand with them.

Solomon walked to the back to give Minka the latest update. He found her pacing in the office.

As soon as she saw him, she said, "I expected more. There are five covens in New Orleans. Five! More than thirty should've been willing to stand with us."

"It's thirty more than we had this morning."

She stopped, her shoulders dropping. "You're right."

He looked at the time and realized that the twenty-four-hour timetable Delphine had given Minka was up. "It's going to be all right."

"It will be once Delphine is dead."

He opened his arms, and Minka walked to him, resting her head on his chest. Solomon held her tightly. "I'm not going to lose you. I can't."

She leaned back to look at him. "What happened?"

Solomon didn't need to ask what she was referring to. He knew she was asking about Misty. Releasing Minka, he walked to one of the chairs against the wall and sat on the edge, his forearms on his knees.

"You don't have to tell me. I shouldn't have asked," Minka said.

He was shaking his head before she'd finished talking. "Misty and I dated for over a year before I asked her to marry me. She was sweet, almost too kind. People took advantage of her all the time."

"Did she know about your family's curse?"

"She had no idea I was a werewolf. I kept that part of my life secret from her." He ran a hand down his face. "That was my first mistake."

Minka took the chair beside him. "Why didn't you tell her?"

"Because I knew she wouldn't believe me. I knew I'd have to show her, and I realized that might send her away."

"Ah. I see."

Solomon glanced at her. "We'd gone to the movies that night. I dropped her off and returned here since it was my night to patrol. I saw that she'd left her purse in my truck, and I called her house to let her know I would bring it by the next morning. But she didn't answer. So I left her a message. I had no way of knowing that she was on her way here."

Minka reached over and put her hand atop his. That small gesture told him without words that she understood his pain.

"I saw five vampires on my patrol," he continued. "I fought two of them, while the other three took an elderly couple and drained them. It wasn't long before Kane and Myles joined me. We made quick work of the rest of the vampires. Except, I missed one.

"He slipped away when I first approached the group. In my haste to stop any violence, I miscounted. I didn't realize my mistake until we smelled the blood. Misty was at the corner, just twenty-five feet away, on the ground with her arm reaching out to me."

Minka squeezed his hand, her pale brown eyes filled with sorrow and compassion.

He cleared his throat that was clogged with emotion. "I don't know if she actually saw us. She was dead by the time I reached her. The vampire had ripped out her throat. There was blood everywhere. When I tracked him down I...did the same to him."

Without a word, Minka slid from her chair and went to her knees in front of him as she wrapped her arms around him. He buried his face in her neck and simply held her.

It had been so long since he'd spoken of Misty. He would forever carry the guilt of her death, but no longer did it weigh so heavily upon his heart.

Minka's fingers slid through his hair to lightly scratch his scalp. "Even if you had told her, it might not have changed anything."

"I know that now."

"I know your secret. I know the truth of you. I've seen into your heart, Solomon LaRue, and I've seen nothing but decency and integrity. You're a good man."

He leaned back and cupped her face in his hands. "I wasn't to you. I wanted you to hate me. I needed it because I knew I wasn't strong enough to resist the pull I felt toward you."

"I figured that part out."

"I've been such a fool."

She shook her head. "Shhh. Don't go down that road. Remember, we're in the present. We need to focus on that."

He wanted to think about the future, to plan one with her. But Solomon knew it wouldn't be wise. Not as long as Delphine still breathed.

Myles came to the door of the office. "Ah, you two might want to come and see this."

Solomon followed Minka and Myles into the front and came to a stunned halt when he saw the leaders of the five witch covens sitting at a table.

He and Minka made their way to the table. "Ladies," he

said when he reached them. "I'm surprised to find you here."

"So are we," said the youngest of the group. She looked at her counterparts and then at Minka. "But it's the right thing to do."

Solomon glanced at Minka to find her staring at the woman who led the coven Minka had once been a part of. The same woman who had betrayed her to Delphine.

"I'm sorry," Susan said to Minka. "I shouldn't have turned you over to Delphine."

Another of the leaders put her hands on the table. "Delphine has a way of making you feel as if you have no other choice but to do as she wants. We're tired of her control. We're ready for it to go back to how it was before she killed your parents, Solomon."

"All of us are ready for that," said another leader.

The last of the women nodded. "Every witch has agreed to stand with you. We just need to know when and where."

Solomon smiled as he took Minka's hand. "Delphine ordered Minka to come to her today. Obviously, Minka didn't. I don't expect Delphine to wait to exact her revenge."

The women rose as one. It was the youngest who said, "Then we need to get our covens ready."

"Also, if Delphine kills us, it won't stop the others from joining you," Susan said.

Solomon watched the women walk from the bar. He couldn't contain his smile as he turned to Minka, but her frown made him pause. "What is it? I thought you'd be overjoyed that all the covens want to join us."

"Susan isn't herself," Minka said as she watched the women.

"Shit." Solomon ran a hand through his hair. "And the others?"

"As far I know, they are. Despite being our leader, Susan could be weak. Delphine must have figured out how to get to her."

"That means everything we tell them, Delphine will know."

Minka slid her gaze to him. "Exactly. There's nothing we can do that will come as a surprise."

Solomon looked at the bar where his brothers and the girls waited. "That may not be entirely true."

Chapter 14

A NIGHT HAD NEVER SEEMED SO TERRIFYING BEFORE. Minka looked at the clock to see it just shy of two in the morning. The boys had shut Gator Bait down before midnight. That's when Kane had snuck away to talk to the Moonstone pack.

Minka twisted her hands as she stared into the night sky. New Orleans never slept. It was a city that partied constantly, and yet the streets around the bar were deserted.

She walked to the window and looked out to where she'd seen Solomon dead in her vision. All she could do was pray that she'd made the right decision. If he died because of her... well, she wasn't sure what she'd do.

A presence came up behind her. With a swipe of his large hand, he gently moved her hair to one side, exposing her neck. Solomon then pressed his forehead against the back of her head while his hands gripped her arms.

"Promise me you'll be smart and use your magic to remain

safe," he said.

She turned in his arms and smiled up at him as she put her palms on his chest. Then she slowly moved her hands upward until they were laced around his neck. "I will if you promise not to do anything crazy. I need you to be safe, as well."

"I think we're asking too much of each other. We will be battling Delphine, after all." His hands came around her back to press her against him.

As she gazed into his beautiful, blue eyes, Minka realized that this might be her last conversation with Solomon. She wanted—no, she *needed*—to tell him how she felt.

She licked her lips and glanced down at his throat. "There's something I need to say now before I don't get the chance. I don't expect you to say anything, but I want you to know that I—"

"Solomon!" Myles shouted from the back.

"Hang on," he called over his shoulder.

Myles quickly said, "It can't wait."

Minka looked around Solomon to the kitchen before her gaze returned to him. She didn't want to just blurt out the words, but she couldn't let the moment pass.

"Give me a sec," Solomon said before he walked away.

She sighed and turned back to the windows, crossing her arms over her chest. There had been plenty of opportunities throughout the day to tell him of her love, but she'd chickened out each time.

Her attraction to Solomon had gone on for months. As soon as she was in his arms and felt his desire, she'd known what had been hidden in her heart the entire time. Love.

Now, she'd have to wait some more. But as soon as he returned to her, she was going to tell him. Who knew how much longer they had before Delphine showed up.

Because she would. There was no doubt in Minka's mind that Delphine would want to lash out at her for refusing to come in the allotted time. The priestess would be swift and violent in her revenge.

Minka looked from one end of the street to the other. She jerked when she saw the lone figure in white standing in the middle of the road.

"Solomon," she called over her shoulder.

Delphine lifted her arm and motioned for Minka to come.

"Solomon!"

Out of the corner of her eye, Minka saw something on the opposite end of the street. A flash of white fur that sped past and disappeared into the night.

Her heart plummeted to her feet. So the battle had begun. There must have been something very important for Solomon to leave without any word to her.

She glanced over her shoulder into the kitchen. "Myles? Riley? Anyone?"

The silence that greeted her made her blood run like ice. They were supposed to face Delphine as a group. Minka turned her head to Delphine.

Perhaps it was better if she faced the priestess alone.

Solomon hated leaving Minka, but he knew she was safe within the confines of the bar. Right now, he had to get to Kane. Solomon ran faster than ever before. As soon as he saw Jaxon, Griffin, and six other weres at the edge of town, circling his brother with their teeth bared, Solomon growled and slammed into Griffin.

That gave Kane the chance to take out a few of the weaker wolves before attacking Jaxon.

Solomon had the advantage of size and strength as a werewolf, but he couldn't talk. He needed to shift in order to speak, but the rift between him and Griffin was now at the point where only one of them would be walking away alive.

And it was going to be Solomon.

"Enough!"

The bellow that came from Kane surprised Solomon. He growled low at Griffin and swung his head around to see Kane standing over a defeated Jaxon.

Kane was glaring at Griffin, his rage palpable. "You promised me that you were going to take your rightful place as Alpha and lead your pack to do as they have always done— help us. I believed you."

Griffin remained in wolf form. He snapped at Solomon, which had the two of them circling each other. Solomon was ready and willing to get the fight with Griffin over with.

"What does he mean?"

Solomon glanced over to find that Jaxon had returned to human form. He was sitting back on his knees, his hands braced on his thighs as he looked at Griffin.

"Griffin," Jaxon demanded. "What is Kane saying?"

Solomon began the change that would return him to his human form. He pushed to his feet and stood naked among the others. "Tell him, Griffin. Or I will."

Several tense minutes passed before Griffin shifted. He straightened and shot Solomon and Kane a fierce glare. Then he looked at Jaxon. "You know Delphine has Elin. I made a deal with the priestess that I wouldn't join the LaRues if she turned over my sister."

"But it isn't that simple is it?" Kane asked.

Griffin gave a reluctant shake of his head. "I was reporting on Minka's movements, as well. Delphine said if I helped Minka or the LaRues in any way, she would kill my sister."

"How long has Delphine had Elin?" Solomon asked.

Griffin shrugged. "She took her a few months before I returned to New Orleans."

"She's the reason you came back." Kane clenched his teeth together and walked to Griffin, who he shoved in the chest. "You lied from the beginning."

Griffin pushed Kane away. "She's my sister!"

"And you should've come to us," Solomon said.

Kane turned to Solomon. "He's how that bitch knew where

Minka was."

"I know." Solomon looked to Jaxon and the other weres standing behind him. "Kane met with you to give you an offer to remain in New Orleans."

Kane released a long breath. "Stand with us against Delphine. She wants Minka's power, which will only make Delphine stronger. We have other allies who will be fighting alongside us. As Moonstones, you pledged your loyalty to your Alpha. Every Moonstone Alpha since the pact has vowed to help the LaRues when called upon. Today, I'm asking you to make that decision for yourselves."

"Do it," Griffin told his weres. "Delphine wants all wolves gone from New Orleans. I can't help the LaRues, or I lose my sister. But you can."

Jaxon frowned as he stepped forward. "Griffin. Do you know what you're saying? You're our Alpha. We follow you."

"Not tonight," Griffin said as he looked from Solomon to Kane. "Tonight, each wolf in our pack gets to make his or her own decision. I'd be standing right alongside the LaRues if I could."

Jaxon blew out a breath. "That's all I needed to hear." He turned to Kane. "I'm in. The wolves behind me will spread the word to the others."

Solomon turned to Griffin. "We'll get your sister free."

A howl split the air. Dread filled Solomon as he recognized Court's voice.

"Go," Kane urged him. "I'm right behind you."

Solomon didn't need to be told twice. He took off running, shifting as he did. All he could think about was getting to Minka. He shouldn't have left her.

It felt like an eternity before the bar came into sight. The silence was what slowed his gait to a walk. Pausing at the corner, he looked up at the roof of the bar and spotted Court. Solomon was about to continue when he heard Minka's voice.

No. She wouldn't have left the bar. Not without him. Solomon peeked around the corner and spotted Minka facing off against Delphine.

"Was that howl from Court supposed to call your friends?" Delphine asked Minka.

Solomon looked behind him to find Kane leading several wolves toward him. Once the group reached him, Solomon looked up at Court to find his brother motioning with his hands to where some of Delphine's disciples were hiding.

It only took a look to Kane for his brother to lope off along with some of the Moonstone wolves to take care of the followers. As Solomon's gaze scanned the area, he found more and more wolves quietly approaching.

Solomon gave a nod to Court and Jaxon before he walked around the corner and came to stand beside Minka. Her head turned to him, a slight smile pulling at the corners of her lips. But it was her fingers tightening in his fur that gave him the most joy.

He bumped against her side as a way to tell her he was ready for whatever came.

Delphine lifted her chin as she looked at Solomon and then Minka with disdain. "I suppose my warning wasn't enough, witch."

"Oh, it nearly worked," Minka said. "Until I realized that you're a liar. Once you had me, you would've gone after my friends."

Solomon bared his teeth when Delphine laughed. He'd been charged with protecting the city from evil, and yet the greatest evil that had ever walked the streets stood before him.

Though he hated to admit it, Delphine was good. She'd traumatized four young boys by killing their parents and leaving them orphans. She'd crept around the Quarter, gaining power little by little so no one really knew what she was about.

Solomon realized he'd failed as a LaRue. He should've paid more attention to the priestess. He should've disregarded the fact that she'd killed his parents. He shouldn't have held such fear of her.

But most of all, he should've seen what she was about.

How many people had died because he'd hesitated to go after Delphine? How many innocents had been crushed, their lives snuffed out because he'd feared the priestess's power?

Too damn many.

And he was ashamed.

His hearing, enhanced in wolf form, picked up on the sound of approaching werewolves. But that wasn't all. There were also human footsteps—dozens of them.

The sound of the bar door opening was punctuated a moment later by it being thrown closed. Solomon looked over and spotted Riley walking to them, stopping on Minka's other side.

"In case you're wondering," Riley told Delphine. "We're sick of seeing you slink around with your veiled threats. Not to mention all your disciples following us around."

Delphine crossed her arms over her chest. "And you think to end it all tonight?"

"To end *you*," Minka stated.

Delphine smiled before she gave a bark of laughter. "Oh, this is going to be better than I could've dreamed. I hope all of you are prepared. You're going to die tonight."

Solomon growled in warning. He was joined by his three brothers, who filed in beside both him and Riley. He crouched down, ready to attack and sink his fangs into Delphine's throat.

Chapter 15

MINKA WATCHED DELPHINE CAREFULLY. SO THE MINUTE the priestess moved, she was ready. The first thing Minka did was deflect the magic the priestess sent their way.

The force of Delphine's power made Minka take a couple of steps back. As they locked in battle, there were shouts as Delphine's white-clothed followers rushed from alleys and other hiding spots.

Solomon stayed next to Minka, fighting any disciple who got too close while the others fanned out to do battle. After a few minutes, she spotted Skye and Addison joined in on the fighting. Riley then let loose a loud whistle, and all the witches poured into the street.

Minka smiled when she saw the concern flash over Delphine's face. Then she held up her hands and pushed her magic outward, slamming it into Delphine.

The priestess stumbled backward. The fear that filled Delphine's face for a fleeting second was all Minka needed to see to take a step forward and give another push of her magic.

Screams of the injured and dying filled the night, while snarls from Solomon and his brothers could also be heard. There was no clash of steel from swords and shields. Instead, this battle was fought with magic and determination of those rising up against a being of infinite evil and destruction.

With every disciple that died, Minka grew bolder and more resolute. She wouldn't back down now.

"Your powers have grown," Delphine said.

Minka blocked a spell the priestess directed at Solomon, who had knocked a follower to the ground. "I feared you for too long. I'm done with that."

"So, you're ready to die?" Delphine asked with a laugh.

"I'm ready to live in a world without you."

Minka was readying to deliver another blow to Delphine when she felt herself flying backwards. She hit the concrete hard enough that it knocked the breath from her. Pain exploded in her head, as well, leaving her dazed and struggling to pull air into her lungs.

Solomon rushed to stand over her. Minka could see Delphine getting closer. She tried to gather her magic, but her body was too intent on breathing to do anything else.

That's when Solomon released a short howl. Minka saw him crouch down. She felt the strength of him a second before he launched himself at Delphine.

Minka rolled to the side as her lungs finally opened and

she gulped in air. All the while, she watched as the impact of Solomon's attack knocked Delphine to the ground. But Minka's triumph was short-lived as Delphine tossed Solomon's huge werewolf body away with a wave of her hand.

The fact that it was so near to where Minka had seen Solomon dead in her vision pushed her to her hands and knees and sent icy fear pounding through her.

"No!" Minka cried and staggered to her feet.

She wasn't able to get near Solomon, though. Delphine's magic grabbed her from behind and began to squeeze. Minka started to struggle even as she heard the sound of werewolves descending upon the street.

But the more she fought, the tighter Delphine's magic became. Minka stopped thrashing and closed her eyes. The magic of the witches fighting against Delphine was thick in the air. It reminded Minka that she was strong, strong enough to break through whatever hold Delphine had on her.

Solomon was growling and snapping his jaws close to her, telling Minka that Delphine was right behind her. Spells Minka had never heard of before filled her mind. She used the one that called out to her loudest. It allowed her to turn and face Delphine. Minka fought back a smug smile when she saw shock fill the priestess's face.

Then, Minka broke free from Delphine's hold altogether. "Let's end this."

Minka could see the wolves circling Delphine as the witches also closed in now that all of the disciples had been killed or had run off.

The smile that suddenly filled Delphine's face caused a moment of panic for Minka until Solomon came to stand beside her once more.

"Yes," Delphine said. "Let's end this."

Minka spread her hands. "Look around you. You're defeated. You have no disciples to do your bidding. It's you against all of us."

"And you think you can kill me?"

"I can. More importantly, I will."

Delphine's smile was slow and so evil it sent a chill down Minka's spine. "You have much power, witch, but there is considerably more you've yet to learn."

"You mean how you took over Susan's body to find out what the witches were doing?" Minka lifted one shoulder in a shrug. "We knew and expected that."

At her words, the witches turned to Susan, who Delphine had been controlling and began to exorcise the priestess out of the coven leader's body.

"It won't do any good," Delphine said. "Susan was weak. She died the moment I took over."

Minka sank her fingers into Solomon's fur. "Your time here is over."

"Far from it, actually."

No sooner had Delphine said those words than Solomon, Kane, and a dozen witches fell over. The witches clawed at their throats while Solomon and Kane whined and growled.

Minka rushed to Solomon as she hurriedly used her magic to release him. As soon as she was able, he shifted into human form. With a touch on his arm, she then moved to Kane. All the while, the other witches were trying to help those who had been struck with Delphine's magic.

It took several minutes before the chaos ended with everyone still alive. Minka whirled around, ready to tell Delphine just what she thought of such a trick, except the priestess was gone.

"She's gone," Skye said.

Kane stumbled to his feet as he returned to human form, unabashed in his nakedness. "Where's Riley."

"Oh, God," Minka said and turned her gaze to Solomon.

Without missing a beat, Solomon began barking orders for wolves to search for Delphine's and Riley's scents.

Minka then faced the witches. "Use your magic. Delphine is somewhere in the city, and she'll have Riley with her. We can find them."

Yet an hour later, they still had nothing. It didn't matter that Minka had combined her magic with the others, forming the greatest gathering of witches in New Orleans' history, or that she had tried on her own.

Not even the wolves had any luck.

It was like Delphine had disappeared without a trace—taking Riley with her.

One by one, the witches and werewolves returned to their homes after gathering their dead, leaving the LaRues, Minka,

Addison, and Skye.

"What now?" Addison asked.

Solomon linked his fingers with Minka's. "We let our cousins know."

"I'll do that," Kane said as he disappeared into the night.

Court and Skye walked away, and then Myles and Addison followed. Minka was looking down the deserted street when Solomon called her name.

"There is the dead," she said.

"They won't be here long."

She frowned as she turned her head to him. "What does that mean?"

"Once a disciple of Delphine, always a disciple. Others will come to claim their bodies."

"We could follow them."

He stood naked in the night air. "Delphine is somewhere no one can find her. At least, not yet. Trust me, we've tried that tactic before."

Minka knew he was right, but she didn't like the idea of giving up. Especially when they'd had Delphine cornered. But she'd turned Minka's attention to saving her friends, giving the priestess the time she needed to take Riley and vanish.

"Come," Solomon said as he tugged her after him inside the bar.

He locked the front door and faced her. He smoothed her hair back from her face and smiled down at her.

"Smiling?" she asked.

"You were magnificent tonight. My God, you make my pulse race."

She put her forehead on his chest, and despite the dire circumstances, found herself grinning. "Magnificent, huh?"

"Hot as fuck, actually."

Her head lifted as she laughed. "I've never been called that before."

"I'll tell you every day."

The smile melted from her face. Every day wasn't a declaration, but it was damn close.

"You were going to tell me something earlier," Solomon said. "I'd like to hear it."

Despite standing in the dark bar with only the streetlights flooding the windows and drenching them in a yellow-orange glow, the brightness of his blue eyes was stunning.

The anxiety she'd felt earlier about telling him of her feelings was gone. Whether it was because she'd stood up to Delphine or because she and Solomon had fought beside each other, she didn't know—or care.

"I love you."

He leaned down and gave her a long, slow kiss before he pulled back. "You've had my heart for many months. I used to think you bewitched me, but now I know I'd just fallen in love with you."

"I thought we'd be celebrating a victory tonight."

"We are. We will. We've got each other and our love. That in itself is a major win." He wound a curl around his index finger.

Minka turned her face into his palm and kissed it. "The war has just started."

"No, that bitch began it when she killed my parents. But we're the ones who are going to end it. She made a mistake in taking Riley. Once my cousins are here, we'll rain hell down upon New Orleans."

She grinned up at him. "Then we'd better prepare."

"First, we have a few more hours until dawn. I plan to make use of every minute."

Minka's blood heated at the flare of desire in his eyes. "Is that right?"

"Oh, yes."

She couldn't contain her laughter when he grabbed her hand, and they raced out the back, barely stopping to lock up before they were running up the stairs to his studio.

Once inside, he had her against the wall, kissing her as if there were no tomorrow.

Because there very well might not be one for them.

Epilogue

Four days later...

SOLOMON STOOD ON THE PORCH OF HIS FAMILY HOME AS the two trucks pulled up the drive. The past few days had been some of the best of his life now that Minka was in his life. But they had also been the worst because they'd found no trace of Riley or Delphine.

Or Griffin.

Minka walked out onto the porch beside him. She took his hand and gave it a squeeze. "It's going to be okay. Riley's family is here now."

"Darlin', you've never met my cousins. They're...protective of family."

"Just as you are."

Solomon had to admit, she was right. He looked down at her. "Have I told you today that I love you?"

"A couple of times this morning."

"Then let me tell you that I'm a better man with you beside me."

She grinned, her pale brown eyes flashing with love. "A witch and a werewolf. Who would've thought?"

"I should be spoiling you with dinners and trips, not putting you in the middle of a war."

She raised a brow and glared at him. "Solomon LaRue, you say that one more time, and I'll turn you into a toad."

"I like her," said a deep voice.

Solomon looked up, his gaze meeting that of the eldest Chiasson, Vincent. There was no need for words. The two embraced as Myles, Kane, and Court filed out of the house.

After the Chiassons and LaRues had said their hellos, and the introduction of the women had passed, Solomon faced everyone. "It's past time our two families spent time together. I'm just sorry the reason you're here is because we lost Riley."

Lincoln, the second eldest, shook his head. "You didn't *lose* Riley. She's a fighter, a true Chiasson. Delphine took her because she's been after Riley for something."

"And we're going to find out what it is," Beau stated.

Christian rocked back on his heels. "I'm ready to kick some Voodoo ass. When can we get started?"

"Right now. Follow me," Minka said and led everyone inside.

Solomon brought up the rear of the group. Vincent came up beside him and said, "Hold onto her. She's a good one."

"I intend to," Solomon said as Minka looked back and smiled at him. "She's the love of my life."

Vin slapped him on the back. "Then we need to rid the city of a certain Voodoo priestess."

"Damn straight."

No one stood against the Chiassons and LaRues. Delphine was going to find out what it meant to fight the combined force of the families.

All Solomon could do was hope that Riley was alive.

Riley squeezed her eyes closed from the blinding light as she came awake on her side. She tried to sit up but was wracked with pain all through her body.

What the hell had happened?

She finally managed to open her eyes to find herself on the floor of a room. There were boards placed over the windows, many of them smashed or rotting. The curtains that were left were barely hanging on, the fabric ripped and so filthy, the color was indiscernible. Dirt, debris, and broken furniture littered the floor.

Riley gritted her teeth and pushed up onto one hand. She refused to allow the fear that threatened to swallow her grow. Because she knew who had her. Delphine.

If the priestess thought she could make her cower, Delphine was in for a rude awakening. Riley was a Chiasson, a hunter of the supernatural, who was ready and willing to fight anything. Delphine was just another evil monster that had to be taken down.

"Bring your worst!" Riley shouted. She then climbed to her feet and dusted off her hands, her gaze scanning the room. Then she whispered, "I'll be ready for you."

Thank you for reading *Moon Struck*. I hope you enjoyed it! I love getting to step back into this paranormal world.

If you liked this book – or any of my other releases – please consider rating the book at the online retailer of your choice. Your ratings and reviews help other readers find new favorites, and of course there is no better or more appreciated support for an author than word of mouth recommendations from happy readers. Thanks again for your interest in my books!

Donna Grant
www.DonnaGrant.com

NEVER MISS A NEW BOOK FROM DONNA GRANT!

Sign up for Donna's newsletter!

Be the first to get notified of new releases and be eligible for special subscribers-only exclusive content and giveaways. Sign up today!

www.donnagrant.com/newsletter-sign-up

LOOK FOR THE NEXT
DARK KINGS STORY
– **DRAGON BURN** –
COMING AUGUST 22, 2017!

Venice, Italy
End of January

EVERY DECISION HAD CONSEQUENCES.

Sebastian knew this better than most. His promise to Ulrik so long ago still haunted him. It was why he'd done the unthinkable and left Dreagan to find some answers on his own. The fact Constantine hadn't called to him via their mental link was worrying, but Sebastian was going to take the reprieve for however long he had it.

He strolled through the street as the cool wind buffeted him. The couples snapping pictures and selfies reminded him that Venice was a romantic destination. He gave an inward snort to the idea of romance.

What had love given Ulrik? Nothing but pain and anguish.

Sebastian checked the address as he reached the building. There was no doubt in his mind that Ryder sent him to the right place. After all, no one at Dreagan was more adept at digging into people's lives than their resident technology expert.

The address wasn't all Ryder had given him. There was also the name of a person of interest - Gianna Santini. Along with her pertinent information.

As the personal assistant to Oscar Cox, or rather Ulrik's uncle, Mikkel, Gianna would know his secrets. Which was why she was his target. And he was prepared to do anything needed to get what he was after.

It didn't matter about the vow he'd sworn as a Dragon King when the mortals appeared on this realm. His protection of them was on hold until he could help his friend. He'd let Ulrik down so long ago. Now it was his time to make up for that by proving that Ulrik wasn't responsible for everything that had happened against the Dragon King.

Sebastian wasn't fool enough to believe Ulrik hadn't done some of the foul incidents, but then who could blame Ulrik after being stripped of his magic and banished from Dreagan, cursed to walk as a human and never shift into a dragon?

His thoughts came to a halt when Sebastian's gaze locked on his target as Gianna Santini walked through the glass doors of the building. Sebastian noted the black Louis Vuitton briefcase in her hand and an Yves Saint Laurent clutch in the other. She handed the briefcase to a man standing next to a black car. After a few words, she crossed the street.

He waited until the car drove away before he followed her at a slow pace. Her pale pink coat as well as her red hair pulled back in a slick bun were easy to spot through the dozens of people that separated them.

He wasn't sure what he expected, but it wasn't for her to cross one of the rii, one of the many small canals, by an ornate bridge. Almost immediately she climbed into a topetta.

His strides lengthened after he crossed the bridge and hailed one of the historic wooden boats for himself. He quickly handed the driver a wad of bills and said, "Private, per favore," as others tried to board.

The driver waved the people away and pushed out into the water. Sebastian sat, but he leaned forward, watching Gianna closely.

"Follow them," he told the driver and pointed to the topetta ahead of them.

The driver nodded. "Si."

Not once did Gianna look behind her. Why would she? Unless she suspected she was being followed. Sebastian knew the facts about her:

Born August 1st and raised in New York.

Married three years to a Native Italian, but divorced for five years.

Took the job in Venice a month after her divorce.

Was involved with several charities around Venice, but always attended alone.

Never had a presence on any online dating service.

Favorite color was pink.

Loved opera and the ballet based on the box she kept at both events.

Returned to New York once a year in November for the American celebration of Thanksgiving.

The Pomeranian she brought with her to Italy died a year earlier.

All in all, there was nothing out of the ordinary about her. But everyone had secrets. He just had to find out what hers was so he could then get the rest of the information he sought.

His driver slowed and waited until Gianna disembarked from her boat before pulling up. Sebastian gave his driver a smile as he exited and pursued his target.

The edges of Gianna's coat billowed around her knees as the wind picked up. Not one hair moved out of place. She stopped before a pub and entered. Surprised, he followed her inside. The bar was upscale and obviously catered to a high-end clientele. The ultra modern décor was just to his tastes.

While Gianna removed her jacket and sat on one of the square white stools at the bar, he opted for one of the small sofas. The place was filling up quickly with a mix of locals and tourists because of the bar's prime location next to a canal.

He ordered a whisky and let thirty minutes pass as he observed Gianna. One man approached her, and she quickly sent him away. Another tried to buy her a drink, but she declined it. A couple of others failed to get her attention.

The more Sebastian watched her, the more he realized she tensed anytime a man came near her. It probably harkened back to her divorce. There was nothing in the facts Ryder sent him about her having a lover. A single Gianna was a much easier target.

He was going to have to make his move decisively. There could be no room for error. He had only one shot, and it had to be perfect.

The moment came when every seat but the stool on her left was taken. He rose and started toward it. His gaze landed on a man about to take it. After a brief stare down, the man quickly turned and walked the other way.

Sebastian climbed onto the stool and ignored both Gianna and the woman on the other side of him. He held his empty glass up to the bartender before setting it down.

Out of the corner of his eye, he saw Gianna look his way, so he gave her a nod in greeting, but didn't try to talk to her. Her shoulders relaxed and she went back to staring at her glass of red wine.

Through the mirror behind the bar, he studied her. It was her hair, a deep, vibrant red that drew so much attention, which went in direct contrast to the Ice Queen attitude she wore like a prize mantle.

She had flawless skin the color of cream. Red brows arched gently over large eyes the color of sparkling emeralds. Lips wide and lusciously full drew his gaze.

The fingers of her left hand toyed with the silver Chanel stud earrings. The white silk shirt dipped into a V at her chest and hung seductively over her breasts before tucking into a pink plaid tweed skirt. He leaned back and let his eyes travel down her shapely calves to the soft pink stilettos.

Sebastian accepted his whiskey and went back to looking at her through the mirror. Gianna kept her eyes down, letting everyone know she wasn't interested in conversation. Why come to a bar then? She was a paradox, and to his delight, he discovered he wanted to peel back every layer to learn what made her tick.

It was too bad she most likely worked for the enemy, because she was someone who appeared to be interesting. Mostly because he never found a puzzle he couldn't solved. And Gianna Santini was definitely a puzzle.

Sebastian saw his chance and leaned toward her. "Can you pass me the nuts, please?"

She glanced at him before handing him the bowl. "How did you know I spoke English?"

"I took a gamble," he replied with a grin.

She didn't return his smile. When her gaze looked away, he began coming up with another way to talk to her. Then he decided on another tactic.

He tossed back his drink, laid some money on the bar, and walked out.

ABOUT THE AUTHOR

New York Times and *USA Today* bestselling author Donna Grant has been praised for her "totally addictive" and "unique and sensual" stories. She's written more than thirty novels spanning multiple genres of romance including the bestselling *Dark King* stories, *Dark Craving, Night's Awakening,* and *Dawn's Desire.* Her acclaimed series, *Dark Warriors,* feature a thrilling combination of Druids, primeval gods, and immortal Highlanders who are dark, dangerous, and irresistible. She lives with two children, a dog, and three cats in Texas.

CONNECT WITH DONNA ONLINE:
www.DonnaGrant.com
f Facebook: **facebook.com/AuthorDonnaGrant**
𝕏 Twitter: **@donna_grant**
◉ Instagram: **instagram.com/dgauthor**
𝓟 Pinterest: **pinterest.com/donnagrant1**
Goodreads: **goodreads.com/author/show/1141209. Donna_Grant**